Fearless

by Chris O'Guinn

Lightbane Publications

ISBN: 978-1490380605

Legal Disclaimer

In dedication

For Kelly. You changed *me*.

CHAPTER 1

I absolutely love to swim. I can't even say how much because no one's ever invented a word to describe how good being in the water makes me feel. Saying it's awesome just makes me sound like every other fifteen-year-old ever who thinks energy drinks and rocks bands are "awesome." I mean, I am and I do, but I've had enough teachers sigh like I'd murdered their first-born when I used "awesome" to describe something that wasn't like a miracle or whatever. I'm trying to not use it as much these days—yes, I am that weird.

But anyway, swimming for me is happiness and freedom and a vacation from being me. I used to spend every day of every summer in the pool, back when I had a house with one in the backyard.

You see, in the water, I'm no longer the skinny kid with the glasses who can't seem to make it to English class without tripping over his own feet. I don't know why walking is such a difficult thing for me. I know that's a skill that most people master before they learn to not poop in their pants. And I was pretty good at it until I turned twelve and, in addition to all the other weird things my body started doing and growing and smelling, I grew a whole foot. No, not an extra appendage. I mean I grew from five feet to six feet in a few short and very painful months.

It was like my brain had suddenly been put behind the wheel of a whole new body and had no idea how the controls worked. I tripped. I fell. I smacked my head into things. It was a riot—to everyone but me. Every day I hoped that things would get better, that I could be suave and cool and all those awesome—I mean, *really* great— things instead of being a total loser. And every day brought a fresh batch of disappointments from the "Sucky High School Moments Oven" steaming like a pile of crap.

Naturally, P.E. was basically torture—state-mandated, unavoidable cruel and unusual punishment. I couldn't hit a baseball to save my life—though I nearly concussed the catcher once, which didn't win me any friends. Soccer was sort of my own personal hell, since in addition to my own feet I had to worry about everyone else's.

Then there was basketball. Since I towered over everyone in my class, it was naturally assumed that I should be a future NBA All Star. The guy who picked me for his team, Stuart, very soon regretted his decision. I felt bad, since it was the first time I hadn't been picked last for a team and I wanted to do a good job for him. But it turns out, being tall isn't all you need to be good at basketball—you need some hand-eye coordination, a lot of dexterity and of course speed. I didn't have any of those things.

Plus, the game is more complicated than trigonometry. Seriously, whoever invented the rules for basketball had to be on drugs. At least baseball is simple—you get up to the plate, you try to hit the ball, you fail, you go back and die of shame. I like to keep the reasons for my failures straightforward.

Anyway, swimming isn't like that. For one, it didn't require teams. That meant there was no one to be pissed at me for making them lose. There were no rules to memorize and no one to compete with. It was like track, except without all the sweating, panting and wishing I could lie down and die.

The laps in the pool were nothing like the laps on the field. I could just lose myself in the pleasant coolness of the water and the way it parted around me. My stupid, clumsy legs were able to manage the scissoring motion that I asked of them without embarrassing me. They propelled me along much faster than anyone in the opposing lanes, but I didn't really care. It wasn't a race. We weren't being tested. I just liked being able to go as fast as I could because it was nice to experience a form of motion that didn't end up with me face down on the concrete with scraped hands and knees.

No, in the water I was…. Well, I was going to say graceful, but that sounds kind of arrogant, so I'll just go with *normal.* And in my life, believe me, that's a precious gift. My feeling is that most people start out at normal and then some strive for exceptional. You know the sort—the football quarterback, the head cheerleader, the valedictorian, those kinds of people. Me, I'd take "normal" any day.

Seriously, normal is fantastic. Take it from Western Valley High's resident freak.

I climbed out of the pool only when the coach blew his whistle and then I checked to see if there would be any lanes empty when the next and last group had their turn. Unfortunately, there weren't, so I grabbed my towel (which hadn't been thrown on the wet ground, so it was a great morning) and sat on the bleachers.

And I shivered. Swimming at eight in the morning when it was sixty-five degrees out had to violate some part of the Geneva Conventions. No one was allowed to leave, though, until the whole class had finished their laps. So I just sat there and dripped and shivered and wished I was back in the water.

Lucas, a guy I used to hang with, was talking to his friends Jojo and Kris and Luis about the new *Dread Fall* 3D movie and how "sick" it was. I thought about chiming in about how I'd loved the chase scene in the beginning, but then I remembered that life was better when no one knew I existed. So I kept my mouth shut.

Behind me, I heard Tommy and Jordan bantering about some online video game tournament that Jordan had won. Tommy thought Jordan had gotten lucky, but he sounded jealous too.

Everyone, it seemed, had their own little group to belong to. My group, the Social Misfits and Outcasts clique, had a pretty exclusive membership of one. When you have as many odd quirks as I've got, you tend to go through friends pretty fast. There's the first meeting, where I'm weird and different and therefore interesting. There's the early stage, where I'm still interesting because I talk funny and have a lot of video games (well, used to, but that's another story). And then there's the distancing, the unanswered calls and the eventual forgetting of who I am.

High school, I had decided, would be different. I wouldn't bother making friends at all. You can't lose what you don't have, right?

Fearless

The whistle blew and class was over. It was just in time, too, to avoid my impending hypothermia. I didn't scramble to the locker room, because that would have been a mistake. And I still slipped in a puddle and went sprawling. Fortunately, since I was trailing behind the class, there was no one to laugh at me.

Locker rooms—not my favorite place. I have nightmares about getting boned up around my classmates. Like, full-on, surround-sound, 3D nightmares that wake me up in a cold sweat. I think maybe it's only that terror which keeps my dick from humiliating me.

Of course, when you're freezing your nuts off, it's easier to avoid that problem. It's actually more of the reverse situation—I don't need to spell that out, do I? But since everyone was suffering from the same condition, no one was eager to make a joke about it. So I was mostly safe.

A guy named Liam had the locker next to mine. Liam scared me. He wasn't a bully. He just hung out with a really bad crowd—the ones who did drugs and listened to heavy metal and looked like they were looking forward to their careers as criminals. His shaved head made Liam look tough, like the sort of guy who might jump you and beat you to death for your ATM card. Under the bulk of his hoody and baggie jeans, though, he was even skinnier than me.

This was the closest I'd ever been to him. He rarely showed up to class, which I figured was why he was a year behind in school. I was surprised he had come to P.E., but then I thought maybe it was a condition of his parole. And then I was very glad I didn't say that aloud.

My self-preservation instincts weren't connected to my eyes, though, since they slid entirely of their own will in his direction when he shucked his swim trunks.

Yes, I'm a terrible person. It's just one of those quirks I mentioned. I like the way guys look and I like looking at naked guys. Sure, there's plenty of that online (as my bookmarks will prove) but there's a big difference between a picture on the screen and a real person. And since I was never going to get naked with a guy in the fun gay way, this was my one guilty pleasure.

The interesting thing about Liam was that he was the least shy guy I had ever seen in real life. It's not like "Penises on Parade" in my locker room. I've read it's different with other people, but the guys at my school are really, really shy. We all do this little dance where we wrap a towel around our waist and then get our shorts and whatever off. Then we scurry to the showers, shower very fast while staying as close to the wall as possible and then quickly towel up and dress again.

Liam was just standing next to me, confounding me with his nakedness. I'm betting you're expecting my next statement to start with, "Of course, if I looked like him, I'd run around naked too" or something, because that would be what normally comes next—I've read the stories too.

But no, it wasn't that. I mean, he wasn't ugly or anything, or covered in tattoos. In spite of how dangerous even looking was, I took in that he seemed average in just about every way. He was just a scrawny kid like me, though he was somehow even paler than I am. Strangely, he had almost no hair anywhere on his body. That's weird for a high school guy, right?

Liam gave me a sidelong look and a smile and reached up and into his locker, stretching up on the balls of his feet as he did so.

My heart stopped. Thus far, I'd always succeeded in keeping my peeking covert. And the one time my gaze lingered a bit too long to be innocent, it had to be with Liam. Here I'd always been worried that it would be my dick that would get me into trouble. Instead, it was my eyes. Is that irony?

I quickly looked away, as if that might possibly avoid the very bad things that were about to happen to me. I waited for the dreaded "fag" to be hissed at me. That would be awful, but maybe that would be enough to get me out of trouble. He could mock me and forget about me. If he held onto his resentment of my lingering gaze, he might get his friends to help him teach me a lesson.

He wiggled as he tried to reach into the back of the top shelf of the locker, and I tried so hard to not notice how that made certain parts of him bounce. Really, I tried. My life is pathetic and everything, but I'm not suicidal. But he kept *doing* it, like he was daring me to look.

I was just glad everyone else had slunk off to the showers so no one said anything that would make things worse. None of them would be stupid enough to mess with Liam, but I wasn't going to be given any kind of amnesty.

"Can you give me a hand?" Liam asked.

What the effing Hell is going on?

"Uh, I, uh…. Ma– Fu– What with?"

"I tossed my briefs too far back. You're taller than me, could you grab them?"

I may only be fifteen, but I'm smart enough to know when I'm being screwed with. "Why?"

Liam shrugged—and did I mention he was naked? "Dude, you're like a foot taller than me. Come on, I promise they're not crusty."

Ew, ew, God, did he just say that?

I stepped closer to get into his locker, but he didn't back off. It should have been hot, getting so close to a naked dude, but it was really just terrifying. The two possibilities were that either he was flirting with me or he was fucking with me, which meant there really was only *one* possibility. Take my word for it. Liam wasn't the sort of guy to flirt with you. He's the sort of guy who would lure you into smoking with him in the band equipment storage room where he would seduce you into doing all the things your mother told you not to do before marriage.

I told you, I've read the stories. I know these things.

So I reached in and wrapped my fingers around the soft cotton jumble of his briefs and told my dick under no circumstances was it to get any ideas as I felt the fabric that had snuggled up to Liam's bits. I handed them to him and stepped back, embarrassed to see my hands were shaking.

Liam was still smiling at me. It wasn't a mean smile either, and I know what those look like, so I could tell. I was totally flustered, which may have been his whole evil scheme. Or maybe he was waiting for the guys to file back in so he could make a big announcement.

But then, I couldn't remember the last time I'd ever seen Liam say anything to anyone outside of his little clique of thugs and dope-heads. So I gave in to the tiny flicker of hope that he wasn't going to rally the villagers into burning me at the stake.

"You're an awesome swimmer."

He said this as I finally got my trunks off. So I was standing there with my swimsuit in a sopping mess around my ankles and nothing but a towel covering me and he was striking up a conversation. I was beginning to think he was even more of a freak than *I* am. The locker room code clearly stated you didn't chat with your fellow dudes while you were standing there naked with your briefs — that you seemed to have forgotten how to put on — bunched in one hand.

"Uh...." Yep, that's all I had to say.

Liam laughed and mercifully put his bits away. "You smoked the other guys in your group."

"Er." My vocabulary had not noticeably improved.

Liam fished out his jeans and a small tin, like one for mints, fell out and popped open. Before he closed it, I saw the pills inside. That made me frown. Yes, on top of everything else, I'm a judgmental jerk. What can I say? I think drugs are stupid. As crappy as life got, I never once thought that getting high would make it better.

For the first time, Liam looked flustered. He stuffed the pills back into his jeans and then yanked them on. His smiling face had clouded over with something that might have been anger, I wasn't sure, but he wasn't talking to me anymore. I was okay with that, since I'd had my fill of weirdness.

I scampered off to the shower and found the coveted corner showerhead not being used—it offers the most privacy. I scrubbed chlorine off my skin with swift, agitated movements. For once, I was so focused on stuff inside my head that I didn't even think about the other guys in the locker room.

I was pissed, to be honest. Liam had been screwing with me. He'd found the one chink in my armor that hadn't been exploited like the others and he'd used it to embarrass me. It wasn't like when people joked about my glasses or my ears or my skinny arms. He had joked about who I *was.* That made me hate him, and I usually don't bother hating people who pick on me. I don't have that kind of energy.

But Liam had crossed a line. Who was he, after all, to make fun of me for being into dudes? He was just some low-life druggie with no future. So he could just go screw himself.

I finished showering and dressed quickly. I was running late. Some of the kids from the next period came in and started changing while I was still tying my shoes, in fact. I still had to get across campus for algebra.

Coach Lancaster stopped me on my way out. I didn't much like the guy. I mean, he was in charge of the class I hated the most. And he had never seemed to care when people were humiliating me, so I didn't talk to him unless I had to.

"Justin, you were great in the pool today."

A compliment? From the coach? Could this day get any weirder?

"Um, thanks."

"I was wondering if you were going to try out for the team."

"What team?" I asked with my usual stupidity.

"The swim team."

I stared at him. It was obvious what he was doing. He felt sorry for me because I was such a freak and he wanted me to join a team I couldn't screw up too badly so I could pretend I had friends. It was a nice gesture. I just didn't understand why he was making it. Like I said, it never seemed like he cared about my stupid drama.

"Uh, no."

"Team could use you," Lancaster pressed.

I really didn't know why he was trying so hard to buck me up. Did I look *that* pathetic? I know a lot of teens kill themselves. Maybe that was what he was worried about. But did I *look* like I was on the edge?

"I need to run to class," I told him and bolted.

CHAPTER 2

I really needed for people not to fuck with me for a few minutes while I untangled the knot of confusion in my head. My day had a routine and it did not involve flirtatious bad boys or strangely nice coaches. It wasn't that I hated change so much as that nothing ever *did* change, so I didn't know how to handle it.

So I was running to my class, and you can guess where that led. It was a truly spectacular fall, full of scattered books, wind-blown papers and a bloody elbow. That made me feel better—back to normal, really. I stuffed everything into my backpack and slunk into algebra just before my name was called in roll.

Things were fine until English. That's when I had my next encounter with Liam. He came in and handed the teacher a note. Ms. Warner read it and then gave him a sympathetic look. It made me wonder what sob story he had made up to excuse his latest round of absences. Some people, I'd found, could charm their way out of anything. Me? I couldn't even dodge taking out the trash.

"Justin?"

I looked up from last night's homework, which I was trying to finish up before class started. I couldn't figure out what I had done to make Ms. Warner call on me, especially before the bell rang. I hoped it wasn't another attempt to get me involved in school like the coach had. If many more teachers started paying attention to me, I was going to get neurotic about it.

"Huh?"

"Could you come up here?"

I nodded, untangling myself from the very tiny desk. I was happy that I managed it without getting hooked and causing the whole thing to tip over. It's happened. It wasn't pretty.

"Yeah?"

I eyed Liam. He was still standing next to Ms. Warner. His hands were in his pockets and his eyes were on the floor. The cocky smirk was gone, which was a relief. I won't lie and say I wasn't thinking of him naked. Remember, I'm a terrible person full of lustful thoughts.

"Liam needs help catching up, Justin."

"Okay."

No, I still hadn't caught on to the reason I had been summoned to the front of the class where people could see me and probably make jokes about my hair or the zit behind my ear or my thrift store jeans or any number of things. I just wanted to get back to my seat in the back as quickly as possible.

"Would you help him out?"

"Huh?" I stared at her. "Me?"

It just couldn't be a coincidence. There was no way she would just have randomly picked me out of her class of forty to help Liam. It wasn't like I was her top student or anything. I doubt she could pick me out of a line-up. Liam had to have asked for me. That was the only explanation. I wasn't sure why. I didn't want to know, either, because I know what curiosity does to cats and I like cats.

I could say no. She certainly couldn't force me to. There was no real reason for me to say no, though. It wasn't like it would cut into my busy social schedule. But I sort of wanted to say no because I would be sending a clear signal to the bald terrorist who had decided to come after me that I wasn't going to play his little game. I wasn't going to be intimidated. And I wasn't going to be bribed, either, no matter how many times he waved his bits at me. I wasn't someone who could be bought.

"I'll give you one hundred extra credit points," Ms. Warner said.

"I'll do it," I said instantly.

Okay, so I can be bought. I need the credit. My newly-birthed GPA was already looking sickly. If that meant playing Liam's game, then I guess I was stuck with it. I could put up with his crap for a couple of weeks until he was caught up on his assignments.

"Wonderful. Now take your seat."

I slunk back into my nice, safe corner. Liam, of course, followed. It was like a stray dog had started following me around. I just didn't know if he wanted my help or if he was going to bite me and give me rabies.

Class started and Ms. Warner told us to continue on with our workbook.

"We're doing passive versus active voice," I told him. "Page Seventy-Three."

As he dragged his desk closer, I watched him out of the corner of my eye. He was like the cover boy for Thug Weekly; with his ripped-up jeans and chain wallet, his black "Ramones" tee shirt hanging on his bony frame and that dark ski cap over his bald head. What I couldn't see, of course, but I knew was there was his little tin of drugs. I was willing to bet he had a bag of weed on him too.

"What?" he asked when he saw me eying him.

"Nothing," I replied.

He pulled his workbook out of a blue backpack that seemed surprisingly new. I frowned, still baffled by the game he was playing. I was on edge, expecting him at any second to make some comment about what had happened in the locker room. What was he waiting for? The urge to call me a fag just had to be burning him up inside.

English class crawled on by. He asked me questions about the assignment, but that was all the conversation we had. For the first twenty minutes, my guts were in a knot with worry. I tried to figure out what he would say and how loud and how the class would react and what I would do after I was driven out of class by being outed as a Peeping Tom.

As the time went by, though, without so much as a sadistic smile from him, another idea popped into my head. It was impossible, of course. There was just no way any human being could be that oblivious. But was there some chance he had not actually *noticed* I was stealing glances at him?

No. I told myself to not even look at that hope, much less think about it. I couldn't afford to let my guard down. School was enemy territory. No one could be trusted. And even if there *were* people who could be trusted, Liam was not one of them.

"Hey, I was wondering," he whispered.

I felt my nails dig into my palm. "Yeah?" *Here it comes.*

"Do you have Hollister for fifth period history?"

I stared at him. "Huh?"

"I could use some help with history too. My Dad's got me covered on math and my Mom's going to help me with biology. But they work a lot, so I could use some help with history."

I knew I was gaping like an idiot, but I just didn't understand what was going on. I'd been the victim of a lot of pranks in my time, but this was one I couldn't quite see the angle on. I just wanted him to do what he needed to do and get it over with.

"Look, what do you want?" I finally snapped.

His expression tightened and his eyes narrowed. "Hey, if it's too much trouble, then whatever, dude. It's nothing to freak out over."

I was sick of being scared so I refused to back down. "Look, I don't know what your game is or what you're after. But I know you're not trying to get on the Honor Roll or anything. So, if you're going to fuck with me, can you just get it over with?"

"Why would you think I'm fucking with you?"

"Because stoners like you don't talk to freaks like me."

Anger flashed like lightning in his eyes. "You don't know me, asshole. I'm sorry I bugged you. I'll tell Warner to put me with someone else."

He got up and went over to the teacher, leaving me to stew in my anger. Under the anger, though, I found a healthy sampling of guilt, which pissed me off. I shouldn't feel guilty for standing up for myself. I had every right. Only I was starting to think I'd lashed out at the wrong guy.

Liam didn't return to his seat. He got a hall pass for the bathroom and slipped out. I slumped down in my seat and fumed. It was completely backwards that *he* should be the one who got offended. Even if I was wrong—which I knew I wasn't—it wasn't like I didn't have any reason to be suspicious. The guy had to know that the crowd he ran with made him look bad.

English class ended without Liam returning. That had me gnawing on my much-ravaged thumbnail. Where had he gone? Was he okay?

I firmly reminded myself that I didn't care. He couldn't turn this around on me. He had come after me.

Hadn't he?

I gnawed on my nail some more. My instincts told me to just leave it alone. He was out of my hair. Even if he had not been out to screw with me, which seemed impossible, did I really want to get mixed up with some crazy stoner?

Goddamit.

I stuffed his books back into his backpack and left class. I could at least bring him his stuff as a peace offering. Then I could put this stupid Liam business behind me. I had enough problems without adding him to the pile.

He wasn't in the nearest bathroom. And I hadn't run into him on the way. I looked down several corridors, but there was no sign of his black ski cap. Passing period was speeding by with no sign of him. That's when I realized I should have just left the backpack with Ms. Warner. Now I didn't have time to go back. I had to get to get to my Physical Science class.

This was my absolute favorite class of the day. No, it's not because I'm a science nerd. I almost wish I were. I mean, I was already a social outcast. It would have been nice to be a brain too, so that I could invent something and be set for life. I would have liked to get something out of being a freak. But no, I just barely scrape by.

The reason I love Physical Science is because that's the class where I sit next to Zach Beal. He's a senior, having to retake the class to graduate. How do I describe him so you get why he's just so, (well, if I can't use "awesome" then I'll go with "amazing") to be around. It's not his sun-kissed blond hair or his dimpled chin, though those are features etched into my memory. It's not even his perfect cheekbones or the dimples he shows when he smiles with his perfect white teeth. And though his eyes, which are glacier blue, are worthy to be stared into for hours, they aren't what set him apart.

It's the entire sum of Zach that makes him special. Sure, he looks like a Greek statue that got turned human, but he was also just the best guy in the world. He never made me feel like a loser. Most people, when told they were to be partnered with me, looked like they'd been handed a diagnosis for a terminal disease. But not Zach. He plopped down next to me at our lab table once the seating arrangements were handed out and greeted me with a big, friendly smile.

"How's it hanging?" he asked when I rushed into class.

I smiled. It was his usual way of saying "hi." The first time he'd asked, I just about fainted dead away from embarrassment. Every day, I resolved to turn the greeting back on him and every day I just barely managed to get out a, "Hey."

When you're in the presence of a god, it's hard to think of something worthy to say. "Please just let me follow you around and stare at you" is a lot of words, you know. And it's sort of creepy.

A lot of times, I wondered why it was that some people could be so cool and funny and charming all the time while the rest of us were lucky if we just matched up the right nouns, verbs and adjectives. I hoped it wasn't yet another genetic thing. I wanted to believe it was something you could learn. That meant that I had a chance, however slim, of being cool one day.

"You ready for the quiz?"

I shook my head. I was never ready for the quizzes or the tests. I thought I had most of the information in my head, but the moment I saw the questions, it was like I'd never read anything at all.

"You?"

Zach showed me his dimples, which caused my bitter, black heart to dissolve into goo. "I fell asleep trying to get through the chapter."

The image of Zach curled up, snoring and drooling with his textbook in his hands made me feel very itchy. He had that effect on me.

"I'd hate to ruin my solid C average," he told me.

That made me laugh. My good mood was quickly soured as the forewarned quiz was handed out. I was sure of about a third of my answers. Another third were total guesses.

Part of the problem was that I was distracted by my Liam problem. I mean, it wasn't like I was all twisted up inside by it. It was really just that trying to figure out what the deal was with the scary stoner was a lot more interesting than a quiz. So I found myself rereading questions over and over, not really absorbing the words, while I thought about Liam.

Why had he stormed off? That was what I really didn't get. If I had pissed him off, why hadn't he just found another partner? Then he could've laid in wait for me after class and beaten the crap out of me like a normal bully.

Was calling him a stoner really that offensive? He smoked weed. Even if I hadn't seen him doing it, then I could smell it on him. I mean, if he was one of those pot activists who want to make it legal, he'd be proud of his habit. And even if not, he couldn't be ashamed of his habit, could he? That didn't make any sense.

I didn't see why he would be so sensitive about it. Even if he didn't like being called out for being a stoner, was that any reason to run off and pout? And why would he care what I thought, anyway?

The more I thought about it, the more annoyed I became. He had no business laying this guilt trip on me. Even if maybe I had overreacted, I have my reasons and I don't have to justify those to anyone. This was high school. I was fighting to keep my head above water. So what if that made me a little prickly?

But I couldn't get his face out of my mind. That look when I'd called him a stoner sort of haunted me. Because while he'd clearly been pissed, there had been a moment where I saw hurt in his eyes.

As I ate my lunch, sitting in a quiet alcove away from the throng of my peers, I found myself facing a question I didn't like one bit:

What if he really had just been trying to make friends?

I couldn't imagine a universe where that was true, but it was hard to ignore the evidence. If I was being completely honest with myself (something I try to avoid) I had been a lot harsher to him than he had been to me.

I had to stop asking myself why he would be trying to make friends with me, because there was just no answer which I could think of that made sense. So I moved on to the question of whether or not I really wanted a druggie for a friend. Was that really the absolute rock bottom I felt underneath me?

I reminded myself that I had promised myself to not bother with the friends thing at all. It was a really exhausting Merry-Go-Round that I had ridden too many times. I just didn't want to go through it all again. Sure, I'd never tried hanging with a stoner and there was a chance that he would be so baked most of the time that he wouldn't notice he was chilling with a complete freak, but was it worth the effort?

Sitting in the quietest part of the quad, by myself, was a keen reminder of what it meant to go it alone. It wasn't that I *liked* working so hard to stay invisible. It was just the easiest path I knew of to keep bad things from happening.

Yeah, that made me a coward. I accepted that.

I finished my juice box and grabbed the blue backpack that had become kind of an anchor dragging me down and went searching for stoners. They had a few favorite haunts. There was under the bleachers, there was the parking lot and there was this little closed off area near the vending machines. They aren't hard to find, after all—you just have to look for the smoke. Sure enough, I found a whole pack of them near the bike rack in the parking lot.

I felt a lot like a very stupid lamb walking up to a pack of wolves with an "Eat Me" sign around my neck. This was definitely their turf. I was an outsider. Obviously, there wasn't an adult anywhere in sight. I tried hard not to imagine how many bones could get broken before help arrived. If Liam were actually planning to lynch me, I'd just gift-wrapped myself for him.

He froze when he saw me, the silly grin on his face fading at the sight of me. The cloud of smoke around him confirmed my accusation, the one that had pissed him off so much. So I understood how my arrival would seem like I was making him eat his words.

Liam, as if in defiance of me, took a hit off the joint he was sharing with his friends. His eyes remained fixed on me as he passed the joint to the nearest stoner. Then he walked over to me and stood right in my face as he blew sweet smoke into my eyes. His expression was dangerous, full of barely-contained hostility.

"What do you want?" he demanded.

I stared at him, my mind completely blank. The terrible consequences of my very bad idea were about to be shown to me. I winced and looked away, bracing myself for the first hit.

CHAPTER 3

L iam's unfriendly expression didn't waver. I felt sick and dizzy. But I didn't do anything. I should have just run, but sometimes I just refuse to listen to the parts of my brain in charge of keeping me alive. So I stood there like I was daring Liam to punch me. I don't know why. Maybe I figured if he did, I could prove I had been right about him all along.

"Well?" he demanded. His breath wasn't very pleasant.

"Uh, you, uh…."

"Spit it out."

As pissed as he was, I noticed he wasn't calling me fag. I didn't understand why not. It was such an easy, obvious slur. And now he was here with his gang of losers, so surely this had to be the time to pull out the ace he had been holding all this time.

"You forgot your stuff in class," I told him, opening one eye.

I held the bag out to him. He took it, his eyes still flashing with anger. "Did you go through it, looking for my stash?"

That idea hadn't even occurred to me. "No."

Since he wasn't going to beat me up, apparently, and my good deed was done, I figured it was about time to make a strategic withdrawal. I turned around and headed in the general direction of my locker. I could feel him staring at me, though, like his eyes were burning a hole in the back of my skull.

"I wasn't fucking with you."

I stopped and looked down at my clumsy feet. I didn't need or want friends. It was just too much pain and disappointment. Loneliness wasn't so bad. Like my dad used to say about other crappy stuff, it's like hanging—you do it long enough, you get used to it.

But if I ignored Liam and kept walking it would be hard to hold onto the belief that I was standing on the high ground. He was reaching out. If I ignored him, then I would be the jerk. And that didn't sit well with me.

I turned around again and chewed on my thumbnail. Liam was watching me. The anger had been replaced by a wary hope in his eyes. For no good reason at all, I now noticed they were a pretty green color. He completely confounded me, and I don't like being confounded. Some think that people are all different, like snowflakes. I tend to believe everyone fits into one of a very few boxes. Liam was a stoner who didn't care about school or his future or what anyone thought of him—that was his box and I didn't like that he refused to stay inside it.

I looked past him to his stoner buddies. None of them were paying us any attention. I guessed, since we weren't holding the joint, we didn't matter to them. At least they didn't look like they were ready to jump me.

Liam stepped closer, though he didn't get in my face like he had before. The way he cocked his head to one side and looked at me sidelong gave the impression that he was worried I was going to blow up at him again. That almost made me laugh, the idea that he could be afraid of me.

"I'm sorry," I told him. It was a total surprise to me to discover that I was. "Look, every day it's something new from someone. Gwen and her friends mock the way I dress. Kevin and his football buddies trip me—like I need any help in that department—and throw my backpack in the trash. Isaac, this guy I used to be friends with, one day he came up and started talking to me at lunch. Then he grabbed my sandwich and spit on it and laughed."

"Dude—"

"No, I don't need any pity. That's not why I'm saying this. Shit happens. I don't even care anymore. I just want to get through this crap fest with as much of my skin intact as possible. So, yeah, I guess I'm paranoid. Or whatever. But after the locker room, I was sure you were coming after me."

Liam relaxed a little. "Dude, I don't care that you were checking me out."

I felt like he had hit me after all; a solid punch to my gut. I stared at him, trying really hard to keep from shaking. The way he just laid it out there, casually putting into words what a total perv I was, it knocked the wind out of me.

I guess my panic was obvious, because he held up his hands for peace. "Dude, I don't care, really. If I had a chance to see Gwen naked, you can bet I'd take it. We're dudes. We're wired that way, even the gay ones."

I wasn't a sexual deviant? That blew my mind. "Really?" I asked in total disbelief.

Liam actually laughed, which startled me and made me take a step back as I prepared for the Big Reveal on the great joke he was playing. Then I noticed something strange. He didn't have that beady look in his eyes I noticed people got when they were being vicious. And his lips weren't curled in that way that suggested malice.

He just thought my being such a naïve twit was funny, it seemed. I was okay with that.

"Dude, it's just looking. You don't think straight dudes check each other out too? We need to be sure everything we got is as good or better as anything anyone else has got."

I knew I was blushing but there wasn't anything I could do about it. "So, if it's something all dudes do," I began, stumbling my way through the subject. "How did you know I…? I mean, what made you think….?"

Liam shrugged. "I watched you in class. You were checking out the guys in their clingy wet trunks. And you couldn't keep your eyes off my junk."

Holy shit, am I that obvious? Does everyone *know?*

"Sorry." It was all I could think to say.

Liam shook his head. "Dude, it's fine. Fish have to swim, birds got to fly and all that crap. Besides, no one's ever looked at me with any interest before. It was kind of flattering."

I let my heart know that it could start beating again. "Uh, okay." I was still stuck on the idea that I wasn't some kind of sick troll for scoping out guys in the locker room. "So why did you ask for me to help you with your classes?"

Liam slid his backpack onto his shoulder. "I thought maybe we could both use a friend."

I really had been teleported into Bizarro World. "Why would you want to be friends with me?"

"My instincts tell me you'd be a cool friend to have."

"You have bad instincts. Trust me, no one would ever use the word 'cool' and me in a sentence without a 'not' involved."

Liam just smiled, like I was being funny. I wasn't. I know, I was being a self-pitying, self-sabotaging moron. But I didn't want him having the wrong impression about me. That would only speed up the process of him cutting me loose.

"What about them?" I asked, pointing at the stoners with my chin.

"They're not my friends. They're just who I buy weed from."

"Oh."

Liam raised an eyebrow. "I'm not a stoner. I just like weed."

I busted up at his little joke. He grinned at me, and I have to say, he was cute when he smiled. It was like this light just burst out of him. I couldn't remember a time when I'd felt such pure and simple joy.

"I'll help you with history," I volunteered, hoping he understood it was an apology.

Liam got it. He nodded. "Cool."

"Did you want to come over after school? I could show you my class notes…."

Liam's face clouded over. "I can't."

I felt stupid for pushing too far too fast. "Sure, I get it."

"Tomorrow?" he offered.

Embarrassed despair turned to excitement and then I told myself I was an idiot. I couldn't get all lame about this. I had to try and be cool. I just wished I had any idea what that looked like. "Sure."

The rest of the school day passed without any more surprises—thank God. I wasn't up for any more shocks. I liked that my life was so predictable—there's a real safety in routine.

My mom and I live in a little run-down apartment. We used to have a nicer place, but then my mom kicked my dad to the curb (and I'm glad she did, since he's a total jerk) and with one income, this was the best she could do. I didn't mind. She was a lot happier now than she had been while married to my self-centered dad, and she was too good a person to be sad all the time.

I grabbed a slice of cold pizza from the fridge and a can of soda and then shuffled into my room. I put my backpack with the day's boatload of homework in a corner and pretended it didn't exist. Then I got out my laptop and surfed the Net to kill time until four o'clock. That was when my Internet boyfriend showed up.

No, I don't really have a boyfriend. But I do have a vivid imagination.

I hang out a lot on this site for gay teens. It's like having a social life without all the work and rejection. Sometimes I just read the articles—I'm obsessed with the advice column and I keep thinking that one day I need to send in a letter of my own. I just don't think anyone can tell me how to stop being a loser.

A lot of the times, I'm in the chat rooms. It's fun to gossip about which celebrity might be gay and trade links to pictures (all very artistic pictures, I assure you) and commiserate about how the adults are fucking up the world we're going to inherit.

It's also fun to flirt. Online flirting is something I can handle. For one, I don't have to worry about the person I'm flirting with scrunching up their face in disgust. Second, I can edit my flirting several times before anyone sees it. Even if I don't hit it off with my online playmates, I can just move on without feeling rejected.

Of course, there's the usual chat room problem. You know what I mean. The Creeps; those guys who are probably ancient—like in their *forties*—trolling for pictures of teens in various states of undress. The good thing about this site I go to is that it's moderated, so as soon as we spot one of The Creeps, we just bring in an admin and get them booted.

The Stalkers are the more subtle cousins of The Creeps. These are the guys who try to lure you into meeting them in some secluded park. They're a lot harder to spot. Some of them give themselves away with the old Age/Sex/Location question or simply "Stats?" but most had wised up by now.

I was pretty sure "Hawaii5*9" was a sixty-year-old dude with a paunch and bad teeth, but I chose to imagine he was a sexy guy my age who had a thing for awkward nerds. Oh, I'll just admit it. In my most secret and lurid fantasies it was Zach. I'm pathetic, I know. But don't worry, it gets worse. Because I have this whole elaborate scenario where we meet and he tells me he's glad that I'm the one behind "JustM3*87" and that he had wanted to ask me out for a long time. I told you, I read a lot. It helps me come up with all kinds of scenarios in my head where Zach and I wind up together.

Hawaii comes on at four every other day and we chat. We started talking a month ago, before school started. I'd never seen him on the site before, and I was

Chris O'Guinn

in a good mood (can you believe it?) so I side-messaged him with a friendly greeting and told him who to watch out for. Since then, I'd found out he was a closeted comic book fan, though our interests aren't the same. He's mostly into the dark stuff like Neil Gaiman's *Sandman* series. I like titles about younger heroes. Hawaii and I have a lot of fun arguing about who the best writers are.

I try really hard to not ping him as soon as he comes on because I don't want to come off as one of The Stalkers—or worse, needy. So when the site told me he was online, I didn't immediately click on the side message button. I have a little self-control.

I got a thrill when he messaged me in the next second.

> Hawaii5*9: Hey! What up?
> JustM3*87: Nothing. Weird day. You?
> Hawaii5*9: Nothing. 2day was boooring.
> JustM3*87: That bad?
> Hawaii5*9: You have no idea. Why was ur day weird?
> JustM3*87: This stoner dude started following me around.
> Hawaii5*9: Maybe he was into you.

That idea had never even occurred to me. I panicked just even thinking about it. It would explain a lot of his weird behavior. But I couldn't make sense of him being attracted to me. And I didn't know what I would do if it were true. So I took the option of not believing it.

> JustM3*87: He said he's str8.

Hawaii5*9: A lot of guys say that.
JustM3*87: And most of them really are.
Hawaii5*9: Yeah, and some of them are bi.
JustM3*87: I keep hearing there's no such thing as bi.
Hawaii5*9: Nah, there is.
JustM3*87: I just can't even figure out how that works.
Hawaii5*9: Some people like both, is all.

I didn't get it, but I didn't want to seem like an idiot or a jerk. For all I knew, Hawaii was bi. I didn't want him to get pissed at me for trashing his orientation.

JustM3*87: I guess that makes sense. I just have a hard enough time figuring out how to date guys. If I had to figure out both genders, I'd lose my mind.
Hawaii5*9: I hear you, dude.

So, he wasn't bisexual. I was relieved about that, though that's probably not cool of me to say. I just didn't want any unknown factors creeping into my entirely fictitious online relationship.

Hawaii5*9: Homecoming's in a few weeks. You going?
JustM3*87: You know I don't dance.
Hawaii5*9: It's not all about your moves, you know.
JustM3*87: No?
Hawaii5*9: It's also about the making out.
JustM3*87: Why didn't anyone tell me that b4?

~ 31 ~

Hawaii5*9: Maybe you should go with your bad
boy stoner.
JustM3*87: Not gonna happen.
Hawaii5*9: Is he hot?

I really wanted the whole subject dropped, so I sent
him a link to the latest P!nk song that had become my
obsession. That moved him off the Liam topic and on to
safer subjects. After a little while, he told me he had to
go do his homework. I agreed, but what I meant by
"homework" was something else entirely.

Jerking off thinking of Zach was one of my few
pleasures in life. I refused to feel guilty about it, since I
wasn't hurting anybody. It wasn't like I was ever going
to tell Zach—like *ever*.

The uncomfortable and unsettling thing was,
though, that Liam's laughing face kept popping into my
head. I absolutely did not want that to start, so I kept
returning to Zach's GQ perfect face. I was willing to
befriend a stoner, but I absolutely would not crush on
one. I have my limits.

CHAPTER 4

L iam wasn't in P.E. the next morning. I admit, I was disappointed. Against all good sense and in spite of my repeated warnings to myself, I had been looking forward to seeing him. I guess since there was literally nothing at school to look forward to, having one maybe-good thing was too much for me to resist being happy about.

I kept looking for him as we collected outside on the bleachers, thinking he might just be late. But Coach Lancaster came out and got class started without any sign of my new friend. Realizing I was investing way too heavily in someone who couldn't be relied upon, I had a few harsh words with myself. Liam was probably in the parking lot getting wasted. A whole day of attending classes had just been too much for him.

You don't know me, I remember him saying.

Turns out I do.

"Today we're going to do some races to see who gets the best time," Lancaster announced.

What did he just say? I wondered, giving him my full attention.

I think I've made it clear that I don't like competition. So I panicked for a second before I remembered there wouldn't be any teams. It was just me against the rest of the class. That was a lot less pressure. I didn't mind losing—I mean, really, is it that big a deal losing a race in a class in high school? I just didn't want to take anyone else down with me.

I was in the second group, so I had more time to brood. I mean I had more time to think about how much I didn't care that Liam had bailed. Because I totally didn't. Sure, it would have been nice to have a friend to sit next to and talk to so I didn't look like the loser no one wanted to hang with. And, yeah, it might have been cool if that person had been the class stoner so I got some kind of "dangerous" cred.

But that wasn't happening, so I was just going to have to deal. It was back to my first plan for the school year—militant apathy. I wrapped my towel around me for a little warmth and hunched in on myself and put on my best angry face. I can't deny that the expression came naturally to me.

I took my mark when I was called. A disturbing image came to my mind of some truly catastrophic accident where I pushed off the springboard and my feet slipped and I fell into the water in a tangle of arms and legs. I wouldn't get images like that in my head if things like that didn't actually happen to me. I did my best to grip the springboard with my toes, just in case.

Lucas was on my left and a guy named Charlie was on my right. We all had goose pimples from the crisp morning breeze. I trembled, anxious to get into the heated pool. Adrenaline coursed through me, which I shrugged off as a sincere desire to get the race over with.

"You're an awesome swimmer."

His words echoed in my ears.

Shut up, Liam.

The coach blew his whistle and I flew into motion, knifing into the water with such skill and precision that I almost whooped in delight. The strong start gave me the confidence to surge through the water with everything I had. I didn't even think about winning. For me, right then, it was just about reveling in the feeling of being good at something.

I reached the edge of the pool, flipped and kicked off. The momentum carried me seamlessly back into my freestyle stroke. I felt like I could go for hours. I *wanted* to go for hours. I never wanted the feeling to end.

Of course, I had to stop. When I had finished the laps, I pulled myself out of the water and pinched my eyes to clear them. It was only then that I realized that the guy closest behind me was a full pool-length back.

That made me a little smug. But that was nothing compared to when the coach announced I was the fastest in the class.

I didn't know what to say. I'd never won anything before. But seeing, for once, the way some of the guys in my class looked at me with approval was quite a rush. Was that why people liked playing sports? Because it made them feel so good seeing other people admire them? Having never experienced anything like it before, the idea had just never occurred to me.

The coach cornered me as I headed back to the locker room. "So why don't you want to join the swim team?" he asked.

He sounded angry. It was like not wanting to join the team was a direct insult to him.

"I'm not, you know, an athlete. I mean, seriously," I looked down at my skinny body to try to demonstrate my point.

"We can train you up."

More P.E.? Who is he kidding?

"C'mon, coach, you can't be this desperate."

Lancaster shook his head. "You may be a klutz on land, but you're a fish in the water, son. Your time today easily qualifies you for the team."

I felt an unfamiliar swell of pride at that. "You know I don't do well with teams."

Lancaster scowled. "Look, son, the team needs you. I get it. You think you're too cool to join a school team."

"I don't think that."

"Don't interrupt." I shut my mouth and let him continue. "I was you, once. I was terrible at everything. I was slow and clumsy—last picked for every team. Then I discovered I was good at something. My something was wrestling. Yours is swimming. Is it really worth pissing away your talent just because you think you're too cool for school activities?"

I didn't much like being scolded by my least favorite adult. I wrapped my towel tighter around myself and glared at him. Soaking wet and shivering, I'm sure I really intimidated him.

"That's not it at all. I just know how the story ends and it's not with a 'happily ever after.'"

"So you're so scared of failing you won't even try?"

"I'm not scared," I told him through chattering teeth. "I just don't want to."

Lancaster rolled his eyes. "Well, we practice every day at two. If you change your mind, come on by."

"Okay," I told him, turning to leave.

"Oh, and I should mention, being on a team counts as your P.E. credit, so you wouldn't have to be in this class anymore."

That stopped me in my tracks. "Really?"

"Yep."

I wasn't sure that was reason enough to risk the inevitable humiliation of trying to infiltrate the ranks of the jocks, but it was a pretty good incentive. The coach might be a bastard, but he apparently wasn't stupid.

"I'll think about it."

So now I had that on my mind. I couldn't deny that I was really flattered to be asked. Over the summer, I'd gotten a letter inviting me to join the track team. Since I had never done track, there was no reason for me to get such a letter unless they just sent one to everyone. So there was nothing special about that invitation.

Coach Lancaster had seen my embarrassing attempts at basketball, though. And he had seen me in the water. He knew what he could expect from me. So his invitation was a lot harder to ignore. But it wasn't that simple.

Being on a team could mean friends and having a place and maybe not being a total freak. Those all sounded good, but they weren't guaranteed. I could easily be the odd-man-out on the team as well, the one people put up with because I had made the team but who they avoided because I was still me. It's not like getting on the team would change who I was—the gay klutz with the glasses and the weird way of talking.

And what if I lost? What if I turned out to be a total failure? Then I'd go from being the weird kid at the school to being the dead weight dragging the swim team down. I couldn't even guess how bad things would get for me then.

All in all, it sounded like a very, very bad idea. There was just way too much risk with a very small chance for reward.

Liam wasn't in English class either. At that point, I just wrote him off as one brief but very weird high school experience. It was probably for the best, I decided. He was one complication I really didn't need. My mom would freak out if she found out I was hanging with a guy who did drugs.

"How's it hanging?" Zach asked when I got to Physical Science.

"Hey," I said.

"Oh, you're smiling. Who's the lucky girl?" he asked.

I hadn't even noticed that I was smiling. What was that all about? What was wrong with me? "I, uh, it's not…. I had a good morning."

Zach's grin got even bigger. "Like I said, who's the girl?"

Not being straight, it took me a little bit to add things up to figure out what he was suggesting. A braver me would have said something like, "Dude, girls aren't my thing." But that wasn't me. I didn't even know how to banter without offending people. Now that was a class I would happily take—"How to talk to people." Talk about a useful skill to prepare us for life.

"Uh, no, I, uh…." There was a lot of stammering and stuttering at this point, interspersed with a silent prayer that the earth would open up and swallow me whole. Finally, I managed to get out, "I got asked to join the swim team."

"Really? Cool. I'd be freaked out, myself. Have you seen the Speedos the swim team wears? I'd never be able to run around like that."

For a moment I was pleasantly distracted by the image of Zach in a Speedo. He could be wet, with rivulets of water sliding down over his flawless skin, snaking around his pert brown nipples and traipsing downward….

I filed that image away for later use. In its place, I put me in a Speedo. And if I didn't already have enough reasons to say no to the team, that one was enough to kill the whole idea. There was no way I was going to subject myself to that sort of public humiliation.

"You should totally go for it," Zach said.

I gaped at him. "I should?"

"Dude, being on a team is like a free pass to as much tail as you want."

Including yours?

I wished I had the balls to say something like that. The look on his face would have been priceless. But of course, I didn't. There were just way too many ways that that could go wrong.

I was completely surprised to see Liam in History. He was wearing a black hoody to match his dark sunglasses and ski cap, so he looked even more thuggish than usual. His head was pillowed on his arms. I wasn't sure why he needed a nap at one in the afternoon, but I had some guesses.

"Hit the bong a little too hard last night?"

He didn't respond save to flip me off. I didn't care. Whatever weird impulse had driven him to make an effort in class and try to be friends had clearly passed. It wasn't important to my life.

But for some reason, I just couldn't stop asking myself why had he bothered at all? And why he had even come to school after missing half of it? It was an effort, obviously, so why was he making it? He still didn't quite fit into his box, no matter how hard I shoved him into it.

Just to really confuse me, he roused himself and pulled his homework out of his bag and handed it to me. "Can you make sure it doesn't suck too bad?"

He'd done his homework somewhere between hits on his bong? I just didn't get it. I nodded to him and took the sheets of neatly-printed pages from him. Looking at his face, I thought he looked even paler than usual. In fact, he kind of looked like crap.

I checked over his homework while watching him out of the corner of my eye. He looked more than tired. He looked sick. Was that why he had been late today? If so, I couldn't really fault him, but he had seemed fine yesterday.

"Looks good except that number six is Ramses II and not Seti I."

"Thanks," Liam mumbled and took the homework back.

He scribbled out the wrong answer and penned in the right one.

"You sick?"

"I'm fine," he insisted. "Just waiting for the Red Bull to kick in."

I was sure he was lying, but I couldn't figure out why. He was always bailing on school, so why was he showing up when he really looked like he should be home? It just didn't make sense. He was really quite frustrating, the way he refused to conform to the stereotype I had assigned him.

Over the course of the class, I watched him slowly return to life like an animated corpse. His color was still sickly, but he was awake and paying attention, at least. I considered asking him if he still wanted me to come over, but I just figured he was looking forward to going home and going back to the sleep that school had interrupted.

So I was completely surprised when he found me at the bike racks at the end of the day. He came up to me, puffing away on a joint, and gave me this friendly smile like we really were just buds. I didn't know what to make of that, honestly. It was like he just didn't care what an odd match we made. In his mind we were friends.

"There you are," he called. "You want a ride to my house?"

"Um, sure."

"Come on, my dad's waiting," Liam told me. He pinched off the joint and tucked it away. I didn't see how that would in any way disguise that he had been smoking weed, but that was his problem and not mine.

I wasn't sure what I was expecting to see when I met Liam's dad, but it certainly wasn't the average guy in the cheap suit that I found. Balding, a little flabby, he didn't look to be the sort of guy that would be raising a juvenile delinquent. He looked more like the guy I bought my shoes from.

We put my bike in the trunk of the old Ford and I got in the back seat. Liam's dad smiled at me and said I could "call him Mike." Then he turned to Liam and asked him how he was doing.

Seriously? A caring dad? I was so confused.

"Well, I haven't thrown up in an hour, so I think I'm all better. Does that mean I can get McDonald's?"

Mike smiled at his son. "Your mom would kill us both."

"Aw, c'mon, I'd give my left nut for a cheeseburger."

I gaped at him. Teenagers don't talk to their parents that way. Do they?

"Okay, fine, but just a Happy Meal."

"Man, lame," Liam complained.

"We could just go straight home."

"Okay, okay, a Happy Meal sounds good."

"Good choice." Mike looked back at me. "You want anything?"

"Uh, no, I'm good."

The fast food reinvigorated Liam much more than the Red Bull had. He gobbled up every fry and devoured the burger like it was the finest feast in the world. Afterwards, he licked his fingers clean, humming in contentment.

"That's what I'm talking about."

"There're breath mints in the glove compartment," Mike told his son. "Please use one."

"In a minute."

I watched like some kind of slack-jawed idiot as Liam took the half-smoked joint out of his pocket and lit it with a cheap cigarette lighter. He did it casually, like it was the most typical thing in the world and not an illegal substance.

"Liam!" Mike snapped.

"Geez, chill already. I'm getting to it."

Liam rolled down the window. That was it. That was all he needed to do to appease his dad. I looked back and forth between them, waiting for the punch line.

There just had to be a gag here, even though I had zero guesses about what it could be. I mean, I was just completely at a loss to explain what I was seeing.

What the shit is going on?

CHAPTER 5

We eventually came to an apartment complex I had only been to once before. My mom and I had checked it out when we were looking for a place. But it had seemed a little too seedy, even if it was a great deal. The thing I remembered most was not liking the way the manager had looked at my mom.

Mike dropped us off and then left. I watched him go, still trying to figure out how to even ask about the joint thing.

"Where's he going?"

"Oh, he has to get back to work."

Liam said this with a look in his eyes I knew to be sadness. It was an emotion I had never expected to see on his face. Before I had a chance to ask about it, he told me to follow him. So I just fell into step with the most confusing guy I had ever met—*ever*.

Liam (chewing on an Altoids) led me into his apartment. At once, the claustrophobic feeling of clutter pressed in on me. The walls were lined with bookshelves, and each was packed with massive tomes and binders and reams of paper. The floor, too, was piled high with the same sort of haphazard mess. The den had a worn couch and a desk with an old computer on it.

A big golden retriever ambled over to us and nuzzled Liam affectionately before sniffing me to make sure I could be trusted. Liam's face lit up as he knelt down to pet and hug the friendly animal, cooing so adorably that it made me smile.

"Hey, Sully, this is Justin. Don't bite him."

The way the dog looked up at me with his long pink tongue hanging out the side of his mouth, I wasn't much worried about getting bitten. I reached out and petted his fluffy golden head.

"Is that you, Liam?" a woman's voice called.

"It's me, mom. And I brought my friend Justin with me."

Liam's mom was one of the most beautiful women I'd ever seen in real life. I guess I mean that she was obviously a beautiful woman, underneath the signs of exhaustion. Her green eyes were soft and kind, but under them were dark rings that hinted at many sleepless nights. Her face was flawless, but it was also gaunt.

She cleaned her hands with a towel and smiled at the both of us. "Justin, it's nice to meet you. You can just call me Anna."

"Um, hi." I looked sidelong at Liam. "Uh, nice to meet you too."

"We're going to take Sully out to the park, okay?"

A brief squall of worry passed over Anna's face, and when it was gone her warm smile was back. "All right. Dinner's at five."

"Hot dogs and potato salad?" Liam asked, and even I could tell that his hopeful look was sarcastic.

"Very funny. The store had a good sale on cabbage and spinach, so it's Brown Rice Bake tonight."

"Joy," Liam sighed.

"Are you staying for dinner?"

"Uh," I looked at Liam and I could see he didn't want to face this mysterious rice dish alone. My mom was going to be working late anyway. "If it's not any trouble."

"Of course not, there's plenty."

"In fact, you can have mine," Liam muttered.

"Liam…."

He affected an innocent look, which made his mom roll her eyes and head into the kitchen. "Be sure to take some water with you to the park."

Liam grabbed two bottles of water and handed them to me. Then he grabbed a Frisbee and told Sully to follow him and we were out the door. Unlike every other dog I had ever met, Sully did not bolt as soon as freedom appeared before him. He stayed right by Liam's side. However, from the way he was wagging his tail, it was clear he was very excited to be out of the small, cramped apartment.

The park across the street was really just a small patch of grass, a sad collection of trees and one very neglected basketball court. I was sure it was not a place I'd want to be after dark. Sully seemed to agree. When this really scary homeless dude got too close, muttering about aliens rewiring our brains, Sully moved even closer to Liam and growled. It wasn't a ferocious, "I'm going to eat you" growl. It was more of a polite, "this is my human so kindly back off" sort of growl. Sully only relaxed when the lost, fractured man was quite a ways off.

Liam passed me the Frisbee. "Go on, give it a throw. Sully needs to run."

He had this sunny look on his face that made him seem, well, normal. I couldn't even see the scary stoner any more. He just looked like a regular guy to me.

I gave up. There was just no way to fit Liam into any of my convenient little boxes. So I ignored the fretting voice in my head that told me this would all end in misery and let myself enjoy the feeling of having a friend again.

I spun and tossed the Frisbee in a gentle arc—which was not enough of a challenge for the expert fetcher that was Sully. The dog easily snatched the disk out of the air and then brought it back, soaking up the praise and love Liam freely offered.

I mean, really, it's impossible to not like a guy who makes silly kissy faces at his dog. Go on and try it. You'll see.

We had a lot of fun tossing the Frisbee around. Liam and I made a game of trying to get it to each other without it being intercepted by Sully. Even when I tripped over my feet, I didn't feel bad, because Liam didn't make fun of me. Though he did laugh when Sully pounced on me to try and wrestle the disk away from my hands.

I was kind of winded when we sat down for a break, but Liam looked wiped out. His pale skin had a sheen of sweat on it. He still had that happy glow, though, laying out on the grass and sucking in lungfuls of air.

"You're in even worse shape than me," I told him.

Liam flipped me off. "I could take you easy."

I rolled my eyes at him to let him know what I thought of that threat. "Your parents seem really cool."

"They're the best," Liam said with such sincerity I found I was waiting for him to turn it into a joke. But he didn't.

"I can't believe they let you smoke pot." I just couldn't stop myself from bringing it up.

Liam gave me a lopsided smile. "My parents don't freak out about things that aren't really important. Do you know that marijuana is actually a lot less toxic than regular cigarettes? All the crap they put in the tobacco cigs makes them poisonous. Weed is much better, by comparison."

It sounded like a rationalization to me—but a good rationalization. "You really don't give a flying fuck what anyone thinks of you, do you?"

Liam laughed. "Wow, you have a mouth on you. You seem like this uptight, stuck-up dude, but underneath that you're just a regular guy, huh?"

"You thought I was stuck-up?"

"No, but other people do."

I wasn't sure what bothered me more, the idea that people had that perception of me or that people thought of me at all. The thought that people were talking about me behind my back put me on edge. I had thought I was doing well at being invisible.

"I'm not stuck-up." Liam shrugged, which annoyed me. "I'm not."

"You like to make assumptions about people, though. You looked down on me because you thought I was a stoner."

"Well, but you do smoke pot."

"Yeah, but it doesn't, like, define who I am."

I felt guilty, which I resented. "Sorry."

"Hey, I don't give a flying fuck what people think of me, remember?"

I gave him a wry smile. "People really think I'm stuck-up?"

"Well, you don't talk to anyone. You keep to yourself. It's like you think you're too good for everyone around you."

"That's bullshit." It also sounded way too much like what the coach had said to me.

"Sure it is, but that doesn't make any difference. That's how people see you. Like you totally ignored Lucas complimenting you yesterday."

I stared at him. "Lucas did what now?"

"He said you made the other guys in the pool look like they weren't even moving."

"He didn't say that."

"Dude, he totally did."

I thought back over the class, trying to figure out how I could have missed something so rare and precious as a compliment. "I think you must have misheard. The only time Lucas and his crew paid any attention to me was when they laughed at me."

"Jesus, dude, they weren't laughing at you. They were laughing at Lucas' joke."

"But...."

I'd been drying off and trying to get the water out of my ears, so maybe.... I felt a cold lump in my stomach as realization hit me. Now it all made sense. They'd tried to be friendly, I'd thought they were mocking me, so I ignored them because that's what the experts say to do with people who pick on you. And what I'd actually done was be an ass to the first guys who had been even a little nice to me.

See what I mean about me being a total loser?

"I told you, people are always fucking with me," I finally said. It sounded like a whiny excuse to my ears, but I didn't have any other defense.

"Yeah, well, we're in high school. That's what people do. But just some people. Some can be pretty cool, if you give them a chance."

Giving people a chance had led to far too many disasters, so I wasn't inclined to agree. "I gave *you* a chance."

"Only because I let you see my dick."

I gaped at him, horrified that he would think that. Then I saw that sarcastic twinkle in his eyes and I breathed easier. My relief allowed me to even muster up an offended glare.

"Jerk."

"So, how do I measure up?"

"*Excuse me?*"

"Well, you're the resident expert, so how do I measure up?"

His teasing grin didn't keep me from blushing to the roots of my hair. "I, uh, I don't know."

"Did you need another look?"

I laughed, completely flustered. He seemed to like having the advantage. "Uh, that's…. No, it's fine."

"Come on, we're buddies now. You shouldn't hold out on me. A guy needs to know when he gets with a girl if she's gonna laugh at his junk."

"That's such a lame word," I replied. "How did we go from calling them the 'family jewels' to calling them 'junk'? I mean, I thought guys prided themselves on their stuff."

Liam considered that. "Interesting point, but you didn't answer my question."

"Oh my God, you were serious?"

"Of course! You're, like, the best person to ask. You can't ask a girl, obviously. And straight dudes would freak out. But a gay dude has wisdom in these things, am I right? You probably know what everyone's packing."

"You're a freak."

"Takes one to know one."

I tried to think of some clever response, something to tease him with to take back the advantage, but everything that went through my head sounded offensive. I was enjoying the strange friendship growing between us too much to want to risk it.

I gave him a sidelong look, mystified by his easy-going grin and relaxed posture. I wished I had even a tenth of his courage.

"It's almost five," was all I could come up with to say.

Liam made a face. "Damn, then I guess I have to meet my fate." He got up off the grass and brushed himself off. Then he gave me another smirk that was, I confess, adorable. "You know, you *can* tell me to go fuck myself if I embarrass you. I'm not made of glass."

"Unless I call you a stoner," I said, the words slipping out before I could stop them.

But even as I was stammering an apology, I heard Liam laughing. I guess I had crossed some invisible line beyond which it was okay to say stuff like that. We were, it seemed, friends. I had no idea why or how, but I was glad. I liked Liam, more than was good for me.

In spite of Liam's dire warnings, dinner was amazing. I guess because my mom works all the time so she rarely has time to cook, a home-cooked meal was a delicacy to me. When I complimented Anna on her cooking, Liam glared at me and called me a traitor.

Afterwards, I did the dishes because that's what always follows dinner at my house. Anna objected, but I told her I didn't mind and I guess she was tired enough that she didn't argue. She also had to get ready for work, so she was grateful for the break.

"You're making me look bad," Liam complained, even as he grabbed a towel to help out.

I just smiled at him and shrugged.

It turned out, they only had the one car, so she had to take the bus to the mall where she worked. That left me and Liam alone with Sully. He cleared a space on the coffee table for us to study on, since his room was apparently a disaster.

Thankfully, the subject of penises did not come up again. I still had no idea how to answer if it did. Certainly, I couldn't tell him the truth. I mean the part about how I wouldn't mind taking a look at his package again. Because while I wasn't really attracted to him, I'm gay and now thanks to Liam I was starting to realize that liking to see dudes naked didn't make me a deviant. It might even be kind of normal.

That was something very *close* to being awesome.

In fact, I enjoyed hanging with Liam so much that I stayed longer than I should have. It was nearly nine when I got home, and one look at my mom's face told me I was in for it.

My mom is not a big woman. Since my growth spurt, I was a lot taller than her. She's very thin and has a narrow frame, so physically, she wasn't very threatening. However, when she glared at me through her thick-rimmed glasses, I feared for my life.

"I'm sorry I didn't call," I told her.

"I was worried sick, kiddo."

"Sorry, I didn't think I'd be home so late."

That did nothing to mollify her. "I was getting ready to call the cops."

"Sorry," I said again.

"Where were you?"

"I was at a friend's house, studying."

That made her relax a little. She didn't know everything about what happened in my life, because there were details that would just upset her and she couldn't do anything about, but she knew that I was short on friends.

"Does this friend not own a phone?"

Her stern look had lost the fear-driven anger of before, but it didn't leave any doubt that I was still in trouble.

"He does and I should have used it."

My mom nodded and let it drop—she would save this infraction as something to guilt me with later on, I was sure. I slipped past her and went to my room, dropping my backpack with a thud. As bad as I felt for worrying her, I just couldn't stop smiling.

It had been a really good day.

CHAPTER 6

Liam continued his campaign of taunting the next morning. In fact, he was *so* obvious about showing off his floppy bits while we changed that Tam, the guy on the other side of him, told us to get a room. I threw Liam a murderous look, which only made him grin more brightly.

Apparently, he had no shame. It was annoying— and kind of cute, too. Now that I was seeing past his juvenile delinquent appearance, I was finding this playful, funny guy with the cutest smile in the world.

Not that that last fact is important in any way. I wasn't stupid enough to start crushing on him. I mean, even my patheticness has its limits.

"Next week is going to be diving and then we're done with the pool," Coach Lancaster told us as we

Fearless

gathered outside. "Then we're onto flag football, so you'll need to bring in jocks and cups."

I felt like he had just stabbed me in the gut. If there was anything I was worse at than basketball, it was any variety of football. I can't catch, I can't throw and I can't block anyone bigger than a fourth-grader.

Why couldn't we just swim for the whole semester? The pool was heated, and the weather in Southern California usually stayed pretty warm until late December at least.

"You look like you're gonna puke."

I gave Liam a miserable look. "I might."

"That bad?"

"You have no idea."

Well, I'd known it was only a matter of time before P.E. went back to being the worst part of my day. There was just no way around it, I decided. Two weeks of being in the pool had been a blessing I just had to be grateful for. And there was always the chance I would be hit by a meteor between now and then. I shuffled over to the bleachers and sat, glaring at the coach.

Liam nudged me in the ribs and gave me a sympathetic look. "I don't like football either."

"Maybe I *should* join the swim team."

"Huh?"

"Lancaster asked me to go out for the team."

"Dude! That's huge! You should totally do it."

"I'm not really a joiner."

"Dude, remember what we talked about? You and what people think about you?"

He had a point, though I didn't like it much. I didn't *want* people thinking I was stuck-up or that I went around feeling I was better than them. That was somehow even worse than people just writing me off as the school weirdo. I could handle being strange. I didn't want to be seen as arrogant.

"I just can't see it going well," I told him. "I'll fuck up somehow and then I'll be even worse off."

"You can't live your life always expecting the worst."

"Who died and made you Dr. Phil?"

He laughed. "Good one."

I warmed at the praise. "Thanks."

I considered the idea. It terrified me, to be honest. It would destroy any hope of remaining invisible. I didn't need or want people to notice me. I knew where that led. The only way it could even possibly not go sour would be if I was actually good. The chances of that were about the same as the chances of Zach asking me to Prom.

"Go for it," Liam urged.

"Maybe."

"I'll kick your ass if you don't."

I snorted out laughter to let him know I wasn't impressed by the threat. "I'm not brave like you, dude."

"So? Fake it."

"Fake it?"

"Just think of what you would do if you weren't afraid and do that."

I frowned. It sounded both brilliant in its simplicity and absurd in its insanity. "I don't know…."

"I dare you."

"I'm sorry, are we eight?"

Liam laughed. I didn't like being pushed, but I had to admit that with him encouraging me, the whole idea was a little less ridiculous-sounding. I chewed on my thumbnail and brooded. In the span of three days, my entire plan for surviving high school had been put into the wood chipper.

I waited until the class was dismissed before approaching Lancaster. I still didn't really like him, but I guess that wasn't important.

"Uh, so, uh, if it's still okay…. I mean, if you still want me to…. What I mean is, if there's still room on the team…." He didn't say anything as I floundered. Like I said, he wasn't one of my favorite people. "I'd like to join the team," I finally managed to say.

"You sure? I don't want you to put some half-ass effort into it and then quit after a couple of days."

He was starting to piss me off. "Yeah, I'm sure."

"Good. You'll need some equipment, a signed permission slip and a note from your doctor that you're cleared to join. I'll get the forms," he said, turning to go.

"Er, a doctor? I'm not sick, really," I told him, causing him to stop.

"School rules, kid."

"I don't…. That is, my mom doesn't…."

Lancaster actually looked sympathetic, for once. I was shocked he even knew how. "Don't worry about it, kid. There's a clinic you can go to. It's not expensive."

I breathed a little easier. "Um, okay."

After I got changed, Lancaster handed me a packet of papers. One was the permission form, another was a list of the things I was going to need like goggles and (oh crap!) a couple of Speedos. I'd forgotten about the dress code.

Liam met me outside the locker room and swiped the packet out of my hand. "Holy shit! I didn't think you'd do it."

I glared at him, choosing to blame him for the mess I was now in. "And now there's no way out of it, either. The coach made me promise I'd stick with it."

"Good for him. Oh, Speedos! I bet you'll look hot in them."

I went crimson. "I doubt it."

"Dude, you need some self-confidence, stat."

I sighed and took the packet back. I had to get to math and he had biology, so we said goodbye. I was still freaked out by what I had committed to, but I was also smiling because Liam had said I would look hot in a Speedo.

He was insane, of course. But it made me feel really good.

I was surprised to find my mom home already when I got there after school. It was Thursday and she always had the afternoon shift on Thursdays. I didn't ask her about it, though. We had this kind of unspoken agreement between us—she didn't tell me how bad our finances were and I didn't tell her how miserable school was. Little white lies kept our family strong.

"No Liam today?" she asked.

"Uh, no, he had stuff to do," I told her, sitting across from her at the kitchen table.

She gave me a tired little smile that broke me up inside. My mom is too good a person to work as hard as she does and have so little to show for it. She broke off some of the grapes she was eating and handed them to me.

"So, how was your day?" I asked.

"Wonderful," she lied. "I got promoted to manager, complete with a fat raise. And then I won a tropical vacation in a contest on the radio." She savored a lush red grape. "You?"

"Great," I fibbed, munching on the sweet little fruits. "I got A's on all my quizzes. I scored the winning basket in P.E. And a group of seniors asked me to sit and have lunch with them."

Her wistful smile swelled and faded. "I got you something. Well, I got me something but it's still for you to have with you." She reached into a bag at her feet and brought out a small box.

"Mom, we can't afford that," I told her, eying the cell phone covetously. I hadn't had one since the divorce.

"It's cheaper than the hospital fees for me when you worry me sick," she told me. "It's a prepaid phone, kiddo, so it's just for emergencies."

"Mom…."

"I wish I could get you one of the fancy ones, hon, but your father couldn't send his check this month, so…."

I took a moment to hate my father a little more. He knew how to push my mom around. He'd done it all through their marriage, always getting his way. Now he was still doing it, depriving her of money she needed just to spite her. I wanted her to take him to court, but she wouldn't do it because of course we couldn't afford a lawyer.

"What would I do with a fancy phone, mom?" I told her, making myself smile. "I barely use the phone we do have. And I'd just lose it anyway. So this is perfect."

I couldn't tell if she believed me. It wasn't likely. She's a smart woman. But she seemed to accept it, like all the other fibs I told her.

"Could you sign something for me?" I asked.

She looked puzzled. "Sure, hon, what is it?"

I took the packet out of my backpack. "I sort of joined the swim team."

For the first time in way too long, I saw her eyes light up. "Really?"

"Yeah, I was kind of drafted. Anyway, I just need you to sign the form. It's the third page."

I regretted not having separated out the permission slip as I saw her stop on the list of equipment I had to get. I could tell what she was thinking as she looked it over: *We can't afford this. How can I tell him?*

"I still have that birthday money from Aunt Judy," I told her. "Don't worry about it."

The joy at my having joined a team evaporated, replaced now with the faintest glimmer of tears. "No, that's your money, kiddo. I'll talk to your father. We'll figure something out."

Like you skipping lunches for a few days? I knew that was her go-to when pennies needed to be pinched, but I didn't think she knew I knew.

"Fuck him."

"Justin!"

I was too angry to flinch from her shock. "I don't want anything from him."

"Justin, he's still your father."

"You divorced him, why can't I?"

She looked down at her folded hands. "I don't want you to hate him."

One of us has to. "Mom, please, just let me take care of this. I want to."

"Justin...." She looked at me with something I guessed was pride. "Okay, hon. But I'll pay you back when I can." She shook her head when I started to object. "Nope, that's the deal, kiddo."

"Okay," I said with a smile.

The number for the clinic that Lancaster had recommended was in the packet. I called them and asked how much the physical would cost. It wasn't as bad as I feared, but it still made me hope the Speedos were priced on a per ounce basis. The clinic had an opening that afternoon, but I was going to have to rush to make it.

"Mom! Can you give me a ride?" I asked as I dashed into the shower.

"Of course, hon."

In minutes, I was wandering through the hospital grounds, looking for the clinic amid the wide and varied assortment of buildings that surrounded Mercy Medical. They all seemed to be dedicated to various "ologies," none of which meant anything to me. I wouldn't have been able to say, for instance, what the difference between radiology and hematology were. But since none of them said, "sports medicine-ology" I guessed they weren't my goal.

I was five minutes late when I finally got there, but I still had to wait twenty minutes to see the doctor. It was all kinds of embarrassing, being poked and prodded and examined by some lady who some kid probably called grandma. But that wasn't as bad as when she asked me questions about my non-existent sex life.

I was only too happy to escape the place with my doctor's pass.

Afterwards, as I was walking back to the car with my mom, I got a little surprise. I spotted Liam on the campus. He was there with his parents. I almost called out a hello, but something about the scene made me hold off. It looked like they were having a really serious conversation. Mike had his arm around his son's shoulders. Liam looked grim. Anna was dabbing at her eyes with a handkerchief.

Clearly, it was a private moment and I would be intruding.

"What is it, kiddo?" my mom asked.

"Nothing," I told her, feeling a knot twisting my stomach.

I took a note of the building they were coming out of. As I said, I have no idea what "ology" is what, but that's what the Internet is for. So as soon as I got home I rushed to my computer and plugged the phrase into the search engine.

Oncology, a branch of science that deals with cancer and tumors.

I stared at the screen and tried very hard to understand what I was seeing, but no matter how much I stared, I couldn't make sense of the words in front of me—or at least, I really didn't want to. As the pieces fell into place, all I could do was hope that somehow I was wrong.

CHAPTER 7

The next morning, Liam was his usual smirky self. He flashed me, just like normal, but this time I couldn't even muster a blush, let alone a smile. I barely slept the night before, thinking about what I'd learned and what it meant. I still didn't have it all figured out.

It seemed like there were a lot of things I should ask him, but it also seemed like none of them were any of my business. Maybe the only thing I *could* do was just pretend I didn't know, since he didn't seem to want me to. I kind of felt like that might be the good "friend" thing to do.

But I had no idea how I was supposed to act like nothing was different.

In a haze, I shuffled out of the locker room, my eyes on the ground. As I passed by the coach, he gave me a frown and a weird look. "You still taking this class?"

"Huh?"

"I thought you were joining the team."

"Oh...." I shook my head. "Uh, yeah, I have the paperwork in my backpack. Sorry, I forgot."

The coach shrugged. "Well, you can stay if you want to, but...."

I shrugged, not really caring. I didn't have anywhere to be. So I just went to the bleachers and took my usual spot and tuned out the coach as he gave the class their marching orders. Since it was Friday, he basically gave them permission to goof off—diving, swimming, whatever they wanted to do.

Liam plopped down beside me, giving me a sidelong look. "So, that *was* you I saw at the hospital yesterday."

I cringed, worried I'd pissed him off—like maybe he thought I was snooping. "I had to get a physical."

Liam nodded, not looking angry. He didn't look happy, either. "So, you figured out my dirty little secret."

I nodded. I didn't know what to say.

"I was eight when I first got sick—leukemia. When I was that age, I thought it was called 'Lou Keema.' I would complain about Lou Keema always making me feel bad."

I looked down at my toes.

"Come on, say something. You're freaking me out."

"I'm sorry."

"Why? You didn't give me cancer."

I flinched at his naked honesty. Now that the truth was out, he wasn't mincing words. It made me squirm.

There was a lot I wanted to know, but I wasn't sure how to ask or even if I should. I tried to find the least offensive question in my head that felt like it was full to bursting with them. I didn't want to say the wrong thing. It wasn't like he had done anything bad.

"So, the weed…."

"Helps, especially with the chemo. But if you can believe it, I can't get it legally because I'm underage."

"Why didn't you tell me?"

Liam actually colored and looked away. "Because I wanted you to like me before you found out. I didn't want this to be a pity friendship."

I stared at him in total shock. How could anyone think *I* would befriend someone out of pity? I thought it was obvious that if anything like that ever happened in my life, it would be the other way around.

I almost asked him why he'd picked me to make friends with, but then I realized that didn't really matter. Whatever had motivated him to reach out to the class freak, we were friends now. And that helped me realize that nothing really had changed at all. He had cancer, but he was still Liam.

"What makes you think I like you?" I asked around a smile.

It hung in the air for a tense second as I waited to see if the joke would flop. The last thing I wanted was to hurt him. My sense of humor was one of the things that got me into trouble with people.

But when he turned to me, he was grinning. "Oh, I see, now that you're a star athlete, you don't have time for us mere mortals."

I waved my hand like I was a royal prince and he was a common peasant. "That's pretty much it."

Liam's face glowed with happiness. "What are you doing after school?"

"Well, I have this practice thing because some guy I know thought I should get on the swim team."

"Smart guy. I'll come cheer you on."

"It's just practice."

"Yeah, but a guy has to support his pal."

I hadn't really thought about practice since finding out about Liam's illness. Now, though, the very idea of stepping into foreign, hostile territory made me sick with worry. Having a familiar face there might make it more bearable.

"I'd appreciate it. It'd be nice to have one guy there who won't laugh at me when I fall on my face."

"Just try to avoid doing that."

That made me roll my eyes. "Yeah, I'll give that a shot."

I found myself just kind of looking at him, trying to figure him out. He looked like a typical stoner, but he was actually a really cool, decent guy. He had this fantastic, super-positive attitude, even though life had handed him this totally shitty deal.

"I know, you got questions," Liam said with the shrug of one shoulder. "But not here, okay? I'm keeping my relationship with Lou a secret for now. After school, I'll tell you everything."

"You don't have to."

"I know. It's cool."

With that more or less settled, I was able to focus on the doom awaiting me. For the rest of the day, my stomach was in knots. I couldn't eat anything at lunch. I kept thinking of one excuse after another I could use to get out of the stupid thing I'd committed myself to. If it hadn't been for Liam bucking me up, I probably would have ducked out of practice

You know that dream where you're walking around naked? Yeah, that was pretty much what it was like stepping out of the locker room in my Speedo for the first time. The only problem was that I was completely awake.

When I'd bought the suit, I'd almost asked the lady in the student store where the rest of it was, but I didn't. She wouldn't get my joke. No one ever got my jokes, except Liam. I'm too weird. Sometimes I think my brain is just broken.

I somehow resisted the urge to cover myself with my towel. None of the other guys were acting freaked out by the swimwear. Of course, they'd been on the team longer, so they had gotten used to it by now. Also, every one of them looked better in it than I did. Especially Jimmy—he even had the beginnings of a six-pack. I'd gone to elementary school with Jimmy, but we'd never said a word to each other because he was cool and I was me.

There were fifteen other guys, and they all seemed good friends. They laughed and shoved at each other the ways guys do. I stood apart, not wanting to intrude. As I'd figured, even on a team I was still going to be the odd man out.

"All right, settle down," Lancaster said.

As far as I could see, that had no effect. Jimmy yanked the back of Chad's suit down, which caused a small scuffle and a lot of laughter. I scooted further away and checked again to be sure the drawstring on my suit was secure.

The coach ignored them. "Today, we're working on endurance instead of speed. I just want to see how many laps you can do."

The guys ignored him because Jimmy was making farting noises with his armpit and that was hilarious. Sometimes I wondered if I was an alien being who had been sent to live among these primitives. If that were the case, I was going to have to have a very serious chat with my parents when I got back to Weirdonia or wherever I was from.

I went to the mark I was sent to and prayed to the Flying Spaghetti Monster that my suit didn't come off when I dove in. It just didn't feel very secure. Or, rather, it barely felt like it was on at all. At some point though, I really did have to catch a break. I was just sure of it.

At the whistle, I dove in and thankfully everything stayed in place. I shot forward like an arrow, and I noticed how much less drag the Speedo had. It made me want to see how fast I could go, but then I remembered the coach's instructions. I set a modest pace instead, hoping I could do enough laps that I wouldn't embarrass myself too much.

I noticed Jimmy in the lane next to me racing along at top speed. My heart sank. Of course there were going to be athletes like Captain Sexy there who would smoke me and do like a hundred laps and the coach would be disappointed and I would be kicked off the team and *still* be out my birthday money because life is just like that.

At least the whole stupid team experiment would be over.

I was beginning to tire on my fourth lap. It was then that I noticed Jimmy wasn't in the lane next to me anymore, it was Bailey. He was also zipping along at top speed, though I guessed he would lose in a race against Jimmy.

I suddenly realized the pack of idiots had been so busy horsing around that they hadn't heard the coach's instructions. Maybe, then, I wasn't doomed to be the worst swimmer on the team. Optimism wasn't a philosophy I had much use for, though.

After practice, which I have to admit I kind of enjoyed, Lancaster pulled me aside. I wilted, looking down at my toes as I walked over to him.

"Look, I know what you're going to say. I wasn't being a team player. I should have tried to make friends with the guys. I told you, I'm no good at teams."

Was Lancaster actually smiling? "I was going to say, great work today. Thanks for actually listening."

I stared at him. "Huh?"

"The toughest thing about making a team is getting them to listen to me. I'm happy that you've already got that part down."

I felt a very warm tingling of pride. "Er, thanks, coach."

"There was just one thing."

"Yeah?"

"Your friend there, Liam? I know his kind. I just have to warn you, I don't put up with drug use on my team."

"Huh? Oh! No, I don't do drugs." *I get stupid enough without them.*

"Good, because we do random screenings."

"All right, but like I said, nothing to worry about with me."

I showered off, mulling over practice. I'd slipped on the wet cement, but stayed on my feet. I had managed to avoid losing my suit in the water. I'd made the coach happy. All in all, I thought things went great. Maybe this wouldn't all end in disaster.

"Hey, matchstick."

It was Jimmy. I glanced over at him as I buttoned up my jeans. The narrow-eyed look on his face told me I was in trouble. The fact that he was flanked by Javier and Kent told my highly-tuned bully-sense that I was in for it.

"It takes more to make this team than being the coach's pet," Jimmy told me with a sneer.

I looked down, very sad that a good-looking guy could be such a dick. "It's not my fault you're so busy yanking other kids' suits down that you can't hear what you're being told."

It was about a second before I realized my inner monologue had become a very badly-timed vocalization. Liam really was having a bad influence on me. I was getting so comfortable that I was letting my guard down.

"Excuse me?"

As I've said, sometimes I don't know when to back down. "I said, if you weren't so busy checking out Chad's ass then you would have heard the instructions."

Jimmy stared coldly at me for a long moment, giving me plenty of time to apologize to my bones for the breaks they were about to receive. Then he suddenly broke out in a (pretty cute) grin and elbowed his friends.

"Funny guy." He walked past me, shoving me into the lockers. "Maybe you're not so bad after all."

I stared after him as he and his friends walked away, completely shocked. Had I actually survived the encounter without a scratch? It didn't seem possible. But somehow, I'd given Jimmy the idea that I wasn't a total loser. Now I just had to somehow keep that going.

"So," Liam said as we walked to his house. "How does it feel to be one of the jocks?"

I shook my head. "No one would ever mistake me for a jock. My arms are like noodles."

"But you're *in*, man," Liam said. "That's got to feel awesome."

"It's not awesome."

"What went wrong?"

"Oh, no, nothing. It's just…. Okay, this is stupid, but I've been trying to not use the word awesome unless it really is."

"Oh, sorry, professor."

I shrugged, smiling in a way that felt like it was radiating up from my toes. "It was pretty cool, that's for sure."

"Okay, but now for the really important question. Who's the hottest guy on the team?"

"Jimmy," I said without hesitation.

"Really? With that nose?"

"What's wrong with his nose?"

"It looks like a hawk's beak."

"If you say so."

"I would think Marcus would be the better choice— you know, if you were into dudes."

I blushed, thinking of Marcus in the shower. "He's pretty cute. Jimmy has a cuter butt though."

"Oh, an ass man, I see."

I really couldn't believe I was talking to Liam about guys I thought were hot. It was completely surreal.

"How about mine? Do I have a cute butt?"

"Oh Jesus," I sighed. I was in such a good mood, though, that I found myself daringly craning back around to check out his ass. "Very nice."

Liam laughed happily. "That'll go great on my dating profile—cute butt certified by genuine gay guy."

"Maybe even with a stamp of approval, like the USDA beef thing."

That made Liam laugh even harder. "So, are you going to ask Jimmy out?"

I gaped at him. "Are you insane?"

"Sometimes. Why? Don't you want to go out with him?"

"Kinda, sorta, but that's not all there is to it. He's probably straight."

"So, he might say no? Dude, that's not a good reason to not ask someone out."

"It's not about him saying no." Though, of course, even that idea was crushing. "It's about him beating the crap out of me for thinking he could be gay."

Liam looked troubled by that. "Anyone who would do that is a moron. I'd be totally flattered if some gay guy asked me out."

"Well, most guys aren't like that."

"Are you sure?"

Where did he keep getting these confounding questions? "Pretty sure, and I'm too much of a coward to find out otherwise."

"Look, dude, I know this sounds morbid coming from me, but you can't live your life being afraid. Live every day, you know? Tomorrow you could get hit by a bus or whatever."

That brought us back around to the subject we'd been avoiding. I decided to avoid it a little bit longer.

"If I was just going to ask some dude out, like, just out of the blue—which I totally am not—it wouldn't be Jimmy."

"Ah ha!" he crowed. "So, who's the lucky dude who has your eye?"

I wasn't sure he could be trusted with my crush, but I supposed I had to stop thinking that way about everything. "This guy in my science class, Zach."

"Zach Snyder?"

"Ew, gross." Snyder was a mouth-breathing Neanderthal who was always picking his nose in class—when he wasn't scratching his crotch. "I have better taste than *that*, come on!"

"Then which Zach is it? I can name like five—no, six—guys with that name."

"Beal."

Liam's eyes lit up. "A senior! Wow, you really do go all out with a crush."

My cheeks were burning. "He's just this really fantastic guy—like, a really nice person, you know?"

"And the fact that he's smoking hot doesn't have anything to do with it?"

I fidgeted. "You think he's hot too?"

"Dude, the guy is so good looking even straight guys want to do him."

I snorted laughter. "You're awful."

"So ask him out."

"Okay, no. I prefer admiring from afar—really far."

Liam elbowed me. "Homecoming isn't far off. You should ask him."

He said it in this sing-song voice that didn't make the idea sound any smarter. "For one, he's a senior and I'm a freshman," I said, ticking the irrefutable points off on my fingers. "For two, he's so far out of my league that I don't have the slightest chance. For three, if I tried, I'd have some kind of seizure and die. And fourth, oh yeah, he's *straight*."

Liam grinned at me. "One, two and especially three are lame. I'm throwing them out. So, let's talk about four. How do you know he's straight?"

It was a very bad idea to even consider the idea that Zach was gay. That could take my crush into places that could totally wreck me. But I knew Liam well enough by now to know he doesn't let things go. So I really had no choice but to answer him.

"He talks about girls all the time. And I think I saw him flirting with Brenda."

"Weak sauce," Liam argued. "He might be covering, trying to keep his orientation a secret. Or, hey, he could be bi. He could just be waiting for you to make a move."

I remembered Hawaii saying the same thing about Liam. Did bi people really exist? I'd never met one—or had I? Totally confused, I just shook my head because no matter what Liam said, I was never going on a date with Zach—not the Beal one anyway.

"Who are *you* taking to Homecoming, Mr. Player?"

Liam's expression told me the Zach conversation would be revisited later. He could be really stubborn about the worst things.

"I'm keeping my options open."

"Oh no, you're not going to do me that way," I argued. "I told you who I wanted to go with, now you have to fess up."

"Bitch."

"And a half."

Liam actually blushed a little bit, which was a surprise and totally adorable. "There's a girl in my bio class, Aolani, but she has a boyfriend."

"That sucks."

"Yeah…."

What I didn't tell him, because it would have sounded weird, was that she'd be a lucky girl if she went out with him. In spite of every single warning sign, he was turning out to be a great guy. I was really lucky he had picked me to be friends with. Who would have guessed I even knew how to get that lucky? I sure didn't.

CHAPTER 8

Liam's room was way cleaner than any teenage guy's room had a right to be, which was strange since he had said it was a disaster just a couple of days ago. But seeing the various medical devices around, none of which I could name, I guessed there had been reasons for him not wanting me in his room other than tidiness. If I kept my room half as clean as his, it would stop one of the regular fights I had with my mom. Sunlight streamed in from the window, pouring over the well-made bed. An old TV sat atop a battered dresser, and beside it was a player and a stack of DVDs.

The walls were lined with photos—some just color mementos of happy times with his family, while most were very artistic-seeming black and whites. The subjects ranged from landscapes to average people to discarded objects like tires.

"I like to take pictures."

"You did these?" I stared at him. "Seriously?"

"Why? Are they lame?"

"Dude, they're totally fantastic. Trust me, I know pictures. I look at a lot of them online. I know when a photo is good."

He looked pleased by that. "When I was really sick, I spent a lot of time just watching the world go by, you know? It all seemed so amazing to me, all these people in their lives doing their things. This really cool nurse gave me her camera and asked me to show her the world that I see. So I started taking pictures. I guess I've gotten better at it over time."

Liam wasn't given to self-pity, but there was no hiding the twinge of melancholy in those words. I couldn't imagine growing up with a serious disease, wondering how long I was going to live, what I was going to miss out on. It made me sad.

"Uh oh, Lou's in the room."

It seemed unkind to make him talk about his illness. He probably spent a lot of time trying to not even think about it. But it also seemed like it might make me a bad friend if I didn't ask. I didn't want to seem like I didn't care.

Liam didn't let me dangle, though. "At first, it seemed like I was going to be one of the lucky ones. I went into remission—that's like, where the disease goes on vacation—a year after my diagnosis. But then it came back when I was eleven. It got pretty bad, then, to the point where my dad wanted to take me to Mexico for some crazy-ass treatment. But then I got a second remission."

"But now it's back."

Liam nodded, looking annoyed. "It's like I just can't get Lou to leave me alone. Anyway, it's not too bad yet. I've been doing the homeschooling thing for years, but I told my parents I wanted to go to high school like a regular kid."

"Christ, you *want* to go to school?"

Liam laughed. "Trust me, when you've been cooped up in your house for years, even high school sounds good."

Sully pushed the door open and came in to check on us. He gave me a few friendly sniffs and then lay down at Liam's feet.

"Sully's been my best friend for years," Liam said, kneeling down and petting the dog. "They got him for me when I got sick. Before I found weed, let me tell you, the only thing that made chemo bearable was curling up with Sully."

I was numb. I didn't see how Liam could be so Zen about everything. If I'd been handed such a shitty deal, I'd want to smash something.

"So, yesterday at the hospital…."

"We were hoping for some good news and we didn't get it. So more chemo for me."

He again just looked annoyed, like this was just such a damn inconvenience and not a threat to his life. Was he just pretending to be brave? Did he maybe not want me to see how scared he was? I couldn't even guess.

"I…." I had no idea what to say. I was completely lost. My heart hurt for him.

"Oh, don't even start Argentina."

"Pardon?"

"Argentina? As in, 'Don't cry for me, Argentina?' Dude, if you're gonna be gay you're gonna have to know these things."

"I'll study up."

"Good." Sully rolled onto his back and Liam rubbed his belly. "The worst part is the way it's fucking up my parents' lives. My mom used to be the executive assistant for this corporate bigwig, but she had to take so much time off for me that her boss fired her. My dad owned his own business, but he had to sell it to pay the hospital bills. We used to have this big house and a yard for Sully, and now we're here, thanks to Lou."

"I'm sure they don't mind." I didn't know his parents *that* well, but from what I'd seen, they wouldn't resent him for it.

"Of course they don't. They're amazing. They're always right there with me, fighting Lou every step of the way. I just wish they didn't *have* to."

"Is…. Is there anything I can do? Like, I don't know, go with you to chemo or something?"

Liam's expression was so full of unguarded gratitude that I had to look away. "Thanks, but you'd lose all respect for me if you saw what a whiny bitch I become after chemo."

I had trouble imagining Liam whining or ever showing weakness. But I wasn't going to push myself on him. "Did you want to take Sully to the park?"

Liam nodded, showing relief that the tough conversation was over. "Okay, Argentina, let's go grab the Frisbee."

"Stop calling me that."

"Maybe just Tina, for short?"

"No."

Liam smirked at me. I smiled back. We'd dealt with the elephant in the room, the one named Lou. I didn't feel better about it, but I wasn't going to waste any more time on him. I was just going to enjoy hanging out with my friend and Lou could go piss up a rope.

As we were leaving, Anna asked me to stay for dinner again. Liam and I still had a mountain of work to do to get him caught up, so it sounded like a good idea. I called my mom, though, not wanting to worry her again.

"It's fine, honey. Oh, but your dad called."

Anxiety hit me like a baseball bat to the head. "Yeah?"

"He wants you to call him back."

"Why?"

"It's his weekend, kiddo."

I'd forgotten. I think I wanted to forget. I wanted to tell my mom to tell him I wasn't going, but then I decided that wasn't fair. No, if I was going to try and ditch him, I had to man up and do it. I just didn't know how to do that.

"I'll call him back."

"Love you, kiddo. Be home by nine."

After hanging up, I turned to Liam. "I can stay."

"Awesome." When he caught my look, he rolled his eyes. "Okay, really cool. Happy?"

I smiled, but it didn't last long. "I need to call my dad."

Liam cocked his head to one side. "Oh, your parents…."

"Split, yeah. A couple years ago."

"Sucks."

"Not really. My dad's a jerk."

"Oh…."

"But I have to spend time with him. Everyone but me agreed on that."

"Wow, you really don't like him."

I shrugged one shoulder. "It's just…."

"What?"

I shook my head. It was such a mess. I didn't like thinking about it, much less talking about it. It made me angry, and then guilty for being angry, and then pissed that I felt guilty and then just depressed about everything.

Liam eyed me for a moment before leading me out of the apartment, Sully right on our heels. We made our way to the park, but this time we just walked around it for a while. Liam let me have some space to untangle the knot of resentment and anger in my head, which I appreciated.

When it came out of me, even I was surprised by how pissed I sounded. "My dad's a selfish prick. He never had time for me or cared about me until the divorce. Now it's like he's father of the year, always wanting to take me places and whatever. It's like he still doesn't really care about me, but he wants to get me on his side or something."

"His side?"

I felt my nails biting into my palms. "When my mom asked for a divorce, he acted like she was being mean to him and that it was all her fault. He still acts like he has no idea why she would leave him."

"That's kind of brutal."

"Yeah, well, the thing that really guts me is how he treats my mom. He's always bailing on sending her the check he's supposed to send. He gives some lame excuse and then lays into her with a guilt trip to get her to drop it."

Liam was quiet while he absorbed that piece of information. "Sounds to me like you shouldn't have to live up to your part of the divorce agreement if he doesn't."

I gaped at him. I had figured he would give me some speech about how your dad is your dad even if he's a crappy dad. That was why I didn't talk to anyone about this. I didn't want them to tell me to get over my grudge. I was very comfortable with it, after all.

"You really think so?"

Liam nodded, looking angry on my behalf. "Totally. I mean, I get it. He's your dad. You don't want to be a dick to him, but it's okay to stand up for yourself."

"God, I wish I had your balls."

"Well, I admit, they're a pretty sweet set, but you can't have them."

Coming out of nowhere, that made me bust up. "Can I just borrow them?"

"Well, okay, but you have to be careful. And give them a good cleaning before you hand them back."

I couldn't keep up with him. Every time I tried, he just got raunchier. I decided to quit while I was ahead. "Why don't you toss the Frisbee with Sully while I deal with my jerk dad."

I watched them run off to the grassy area and then punched in my dad's number. I felt like there were hamsters running on a wheel in my gut as it rang again and again. What would I do if I had to leave a message?"

"Hello?"

"Hey, dad."

"Justin! How's it going, champ?"

"Uh, fine...."

"There's a Bond film marathon at the Cerritos Megaplex on Saturday. That sound like fun?"

It kind of did, really. And this was what I really resented about my dad. It was so easy to be angry with him until you talked to him. Then it felt like yelling at a little kid. Sometimes I really didn't think he even understood why the things he did were wrong.

"Uh, well...."

"Come on, we'll pig out on junk food and you can try to convince me Brosnan is better than Connery."

"I...."

I looked across the park and saw Liam running around and having fun with Sully. I remembered what he told me about how to fake being brave. If ever there were a time to give it a try, it was right then.

"I don't think so, Dad."

There was a moment's pause. "That sucks. I thought you like Bond movies."

"I do, but—"

"You don't want to sit in a theater for ten hours? We can leave early or go late."

"No, Dad—"

"Or we could do the marathon at home. Then we'd get to pick—"

"Dad!"

"What?"

"Why didn't you send Mom the check this month?" I ran a shaking hand through my hair.

"Champ, you don't need to worry about that."

"I do, when it means we have to choose between electricity and food."

"Is it that bad?" my dad asked, sounding totally shocked. "You could always stay with me...."

The anger returned, so suddenly it made me tremble. "Is *that* what this stupid game is about?"

"Huh?"

"Are you trying to make things so bad at Mom's that I'll move…." I felt shockwaves of realization hit me. "Or is it so that *she'll* take you back?"

"Don't be silly, sport. Some clients were late with their payments this month is all."

"You always say that," I said, and even I could hear the growl in my voice. "But then when those checks come in, it's not like you make it up to Mom. You've never sent two payments at once, not ever."

"Son, I have bills to pay too."

Now he was sulking. This was what usually did my mom in. She just couldn't handle it when he pouted. I hadn't had much success against it either. It just felt so *bad* to call him on his crap.

"Whatever," I told him. "But until you send the check, I'm not coming over."

"Did your mother put you up to this?"

I got even more pissed. "You know she wouldn't. I'll get an earful for doing this, but I don't care. You stop jerking her around and I'll do the visits, but not until."

"You're not being fair."

"Yeah, well, newsflash: life's not fair. Now, I'm chewing up minutes, so I have to go."

"Son—"

"Later."

I sat on a nearby bench and stared at the phone. I felt really good for having made a stand, and yet I felt like crap for having been so harsh to my dad. All these confusing feelings chased each other in my head, guilt and relief, anger and sadness. It had been a rollercoaster of a day.

Sully appeared before me, Frisbee held in his jaws and hope lighting up his eyes. I looked up at Liam, feeling stupid (on top of everything else) for letting this get to me when he had so many worse things to handle.

He didn't seem to agree. He reached out and gripped my shoulder and gave me a supportive smile. "Wanna help me wear Sully out?" he asked.

"Yeah," I told him.

I had to force the smile, but I really was grateful to him. He'd helped me do something that I had badly needed to do. So I followed him back to the grassy area and made myself focus on having fun instead of the shit storm I had just stirred up.

CHAPTER 9

It turned out the consequences of my actions weren't very far off. In fact, they were waiting for me when I got home.

"You need to call your father."

"Hi, mom, how are you?"

She glared at me, and it wasn't one of her mock-glares either. She was pissed. "Don't get smart with me, kiddo. Your father called and he was furious. He yelled at me and accused me of turning you against him."

"He shouldn't have done that."

"It took me ten minutes just to figure out what he was talking about."

I guess I should have warned her. Somehow, I hadn't thought my dad would call her instead of me. I forgot to take into account, though, that he could still intimidate her.

"It's not that big of a deal."

"Not…. Kiddo, these visits are part of the agreement. If I don't live up to my part, he can take me to court."

"Good, then he can explain to a judge why he doesn't send the checks like he's supposed to."

"Justin…" Her anger evaporated and she looked away. "That's not…. You don't need to worry about that."

"Of course I do."

"Kiddo, I'm sorry you don't have all the things you used to have. I know we're having a tough time."

"Mom, I don't care about stuff!" I told her. "You're doing everything you can. He should too."

My mom's eyes were gleaming with tears. "I don't want you to feel like you have to fix things."

I felt like crap. I hated seeing her cry and even though I knew—*knew*—it was my dad's fault, I still felt guilty. "Mom, look…. I don't want to see him, okay? The judge said I could make that call when I'm sixteen. I'm a few months early, is all."

"Nearly a year, actually."

"I'm rounding," I told her with a wry smile.

She surprised me by pulling me into a hug. "You're a good kid, Justin."

"Does that mean I don't have to clean my room?"

She smiled faintly, holding me at arm's length. "But it's a pigsty."

"Do the pigs really mind, though? I mean, has anyone asked the pigs how they feel about the sty?"

I got the briefest laugh out of her. "I just worry, you know? I don't want you to look back someday and wish you'd been closer to your dad."

"Well, I'll worry about that when it happens."

She got a napkin and dried her eyes. "So, when do I get to meet this Liam?"

"Oh, I don't know. Hadn't really thought about it."

I *had* thought about it. I'd imagined her coming into my room while Liam was smoking a joint and beating me within an inch of my life. As yet, I hadn't figured out how to introduce them so I was planning to avoid it.

"We should have him over for dinner some night. His parents are feeding you more than I am."

That could work. Liam adored junk food, so he'd probably love having the take out we usually ate. I wasn't sure how bad that would be for him, though. I'd have to ask him.

I finally made my way to my room and firmly shut the door. I got online to check my favorite site for messages. It was usually spam or just annoying announcements from the site admins. Sometimes the Creeps sent me pictures that I didn't need to see. As yet, I had not gotten the note from Zach that I dreamed about.

Hawaii was on, to my surprise. Even more surprising, he pinged me.

Hawaii5*9: Yo! Where you been? Haven't seen you in a while.

I liked that he had been looking for me.

JustM3*87: I just had some stuff going on. I joined the swim team.
Hawaii5*9: Really?
JustM3*87: I know, right? It's like a sign of the apocalypse.

Hawaii5*9: LOL What race you gonna do?

JustM3*87: ??

Hawaii5*9: You know, breaststroke, backstroke…?

JustM3*87: I have no idea.

Hawaii5*9: Well, congrats!

JustM3*87: Thx

Hawaii5*9: How are things going with your new bf?

JustM3*87: ??

Hawaii5*9: That stoner who was stalking you.

JustM3*87: :) His name's Liam. He's cool. And he's not my bf.

Hawaii5*9: Rly?

JustM3*87: Srs.

Hawaii5*9: Kewl. So, have you read Dreamscape yet?

JustM3*87: Oh yeah….

I had a lot of fun debating the comic with him. Of course, he loved it and I kind of did too, but it was fun to poke holes in the plot just to watch him fume. I didn't feel bad about teasing him, either. He did it to me with the titles I made him read.

While it was fun, I noticed something weird that had never happened before. As much as I liked chatting with Hawaii, I kept thinking about Liam. I wanted to call him and chat with him, which was really lame since I'd only left him like a half hour ago.

JustM3*87: So, did you hear about the Bond marathon?

Hawaii5*9: Yes! I so want to go. No one to go with, though. :(

Chris O'Guinn

I had this crazy idea of asking him to go with me. There was just no way, though. For one, I couldn't afford it, not without Aunt Judy's birthday money. And for second, of course, there was the fact that Hawaii wasn't actually a teenager. He was some creepy old guy waiting for the chance to do things to me that are not G-rated. I had to remember where the line between fantasy and reality was.

> JustM3*87: I'm tapped out after buying all that swim gear.
> Hawaii5*9: That sucks. I gtg, it's family Monopoly night. *eyeroll* l8r!

I signed off and then started sorting through pictures on my hard drive. They weren't as artistic as the ones Liam took, but they made me think of him anyway. I wished I had the money for the Bond marathon so I could go with him. It would be lots of fun, I figured, and way better than going with my dad.

Yes, so I had a crush on him. I know I said I wouldn't, and I didn't mean to. It just sort of happened. He was the coolest guy I had ever met. I was even willing to put him a notch above Zach, so you know I liked him a whole lot. I guess part of it was that I had never met anyone like him before in my life.

But when I had a dream about him that night—a full HD, surround-sound scene in which not an article of clothing was ever spotted, I was a little unsettled. I didn't like the notion that my sub-conscious was getting ideas of its own.

Nor did I know what to think of the fact that it was the most intense sex dream I had ever had.

I tried to tell myself that it was just part of the wonderfully weird experience of adolescence and to not read anything into it. But it made me uncomfortable around Liam, when I went over to his house the next day. It was totally insane, but I was scared he might somehow realize I'd been thinking those things.

"I've got some stuff to show you," he said after we got back from walking Sully.

"Yeah?"

Liam nodded, leading me to his room. While his computer booted up, he rolled himself a joint. I didn't even blink an eye anymore. Weed was just one of his quirks—like the extremely embarrassing questions he liked to ask.

Instead, I started going through his stuff. He had just about every DVD ever made, it seemed. A few of the cases looked more worn than others, hinting those were the movies he liked best.

"Oh, a Harry Potter fan," I teased.

Liam flipped me off. "Harry is the fucking man, okay?"

I snickered. "If you say so. I gave up after the first one."

Liam's face scrunched up. "Wait, you've never seen the movies or read the books?"

"I watched the first movie and I was bored."

"Okay, well, we'll fix that later."

I moved onto his bookshelf. One whole bookcase was dedicated to horror. I'd never been a fan of horror books. The broken spines on the paperbacks told me they had been read several times. I was about to ask him which was his favorite when he excused himself to go to the bathroom.

The next bookshelf was dedicated to photography books. He had books devoted to single artists like Ansel Adams and Annie Liebovitz. He had books dedicated to places, like various state parks, the rain forests, as well as the tropics of Hawaii, the mountains of Washington and the deserts of New Mexico.

"Those are places I want to go to," he told me when he got back. "Especially Hawaii. It's supposed to be one of the most gorgeous places on Earth."

I thumbed through the pages of one of the Hawaii books. "Sounds fantastic."

"It will be. Come on, let me show you this so we can watch movies."

He was bouncing on his heels, waving me over to his computer. I took a seat and he brought up a really cool photo of a scene I recognized. It was the swim team, and they were laughing. Jimmy wasn't in the picture though. So it just looked like boys having a good time. He had rendered it in black and white, so it looked really classy.

"You took pictures of us?"

"Is that okay?"

I shrugged, not really seeing a problem unless I was in any of them. With luck, his artistic eye would edit me out if that happened. I clicked through to the next photo and then the next, completely fascinated by what I was seeing. He had taken practice, which had been too terrifying to me to be interesting, and made it into art. Each frozen moment was like a tiny story all on its own.

"I call the next one 'Fearless.'"

I stared at it. I couldn't even believe what I was seeing. He had caught me in mid-flight, leaping through the air towards the water. My face was serene. My body formed a perfect arc. It was me, but it wasn't me. It was, I realized, how Liam saw me.

"Wow." I couldn't stop staring.

"It's okay?"

I gaped at him. "Dude, you should work at a magazine or something. Anyone who can make me look good is a miracle worker."

"Hardly." Liam beamed at me. "But I'm glad you like it."

"It's amazing."

Now Liam was blushing under the praise. "Well, it's okay. I messed up the crop and the angle—"

"Shut up," I told him. "It's great."

"Okay." He squirmed. "Now, it's time for you to meet my man Harry."

I groaned, only I didn't really mind. It wasn't the Bond marathon, but it was almost better. Liam was so into the movies, watching his reactions was actually the best part. He would pause the movie every few minutes to explain something to me from the books or just to remark on something cool in the scene.

After the fourth movie, I was exhausted and had to go home. But we agreed to pick up on Sunday, so he could finish my "education."

CHAPTER 10

My preferred locale for lunch was away from the busy quad where most everyone ate. It was located between two of the buildings, which made it nice and quiet. It had taken me a while to scope it out and determine that it was the best place for privacy and security. I could curl up with my book and my bologna sandwich and not worry about being bothered.

So it was kind of a big deal that I had invited Liam to share it with me. I wasn't sure if he got it, and I know it would have seemed weird if I had tried to explain it. Some things only really make sense in my head.

"How was diving?"

"Terrifying," Liam said, eating his hummus and tomato sandwich without enthusiasm.

"Yeah?"

"Seriously. You get up there and you look down and the pool looks so small and it seems like if you jump too far, you'll splatter all over the pavement."

"I probably would."

Liam elbowed me. "Shut up."

I shrugged. "Sorry."

"Luis lost his suit, though, so that was funny."

"At least for everyone but Luis."

"Actually, he was laughing the hardest. He was getting ready to throw his suit in first on his next dive, but the coach told him he'd send him to the principal if he did that."

What a gift that would be, to be able to laugh at your own embarrassing moments. I was seriously jealous. "If that had happened to me, I would have transferred schools."

"Then who would I have to talk to?"

I thought it was weird that he would think he would have a hard time making friends. He was the most likable guy I had ever met. I didn't think anyone could resist his charms.

"My mom thinks I'm making you up."

"What now?" he asked, forcing down the last bite of his sandwich.

The next thing out of his bag was a pack of trail mix. He looked positively forlorn, like he couldn't imagine why his mother would do that to him. He eyed my Cheetos so covetously that I had to offer him a few.

"She wants to meet you."

"Oh, that's cool."

"Uh, well, maybe not. My mom's great, but she's not exactly open-minded."

"Okay."

"So, you couldn't, you know...."

Liam laughed. "Dude, I'm not going to toke up in your house!"

It was weird to me that I felt bad about having to ask him to conceal his pot habit. It shouldn't be strange to ask your friend to refrain from using illegal substances at your house. But I guess I didn't want to put him out or something.

"I know you need it, for, you know, Lou."

"I'm not always high, you know. I can go an afternoon without a date with Mary Jane."

Now I felt bad for making him think I still saw him as a stoner. "No, dude, no, I know. I just don't want you to need it and not be able to have it."

"I'll be fine, but thanks for worrying."

"Worrying comes naturally."

"I've noticed." He gave me a sidelong look. "Can I ask you something?"

"Sure."

"Do your parents know?"

"Know what?"

"That you're gay."

"Oh, *hell* no." I shuddered. "I'd know if they knew, because I'd be dead and buried and this doesn't look like the afterlife."

Liam frowned. "Doesn't that kind of suck? Not being honest with them?"

"I prefer to think of it more as protecting them from things they can't handle."

"You sure they can't handle it?"

I nodded. "Very. My dad's a big, immature kid. He loves to make really horrible jokes about gays. And my mom voted for that thing to ban gay marriage. If they found out their son is a homo? They'd freak."

"That sucks," he agreed. "But maybe they'd change their minds about it all if they knew you were gay."

"Not a gamble I want to take. My mom and I have a relationship built on a solid foundation of lies of omission. I see no reason to change that."

"Your call," he conceded.

"I appreciate—"

My words stopped flowing as I caught sight of Zach. He seemed to be coming from the parking lot, so I guessed he'd been off campus for lunch. He was alone, walking along with an easy, confident stride. He had his ear-buds in, and I could see his lips moving a little as he murmured the words to the song he was listening to.

Liam turned to see what I was looking at. "Oh, it's Mr. Stud Ranger."

"Shut up," I replied. *Stud Ranger?*

"You should ask him out."

"We had this conversation."

"Yes, and I won," Liam argued.

"That's not how I remember it."

Liam threw me a grin that, mixed with the sparkle in his eye, told me I was in trouble. "Okay, Chicken Boy, time for your wing man to fly into action."

I had no idea what he meant and he was gone before I had the slightest clue what he was talking about. I watched in helpless horror as he walked right up to Zach and started talking to him. I couldn't hear the words, which was maddening. Was Liam telling Zach I was into him? Was he outing me? What was going on?

I couldn't do anything, though. Much as a part of me wanted to drag Liam back by the scruff and make him promise to never do anything like this ever again, there was no way to do that without making the situation even more awkward. So all I could do was sit and watch and chew on my ragged thumb nail and panic.

Liam strolled on back to me, smirking in that adorable way of his, but I was too pissed to be distracted by his cuteness. I was going to kill him!

Zach, I noticed, had gone on his merry way.

"He's straight, or so he says," Liam remarked as he sat down again.

"What did you *say*?" I demanded. How could he be this casual about these things?

"I asked him if he was gay or bi, is all. He said he's straight and asked if I was hitting on him. I said I wasn't, that I was asking for a friend."

I stared at Liam. It was the nicest, bravest thing anyone had ever done for me. He was completely insane and had no respect for the rules of high school, but I couldn't get past how incredibly sweet it was.

So I decided to not kill him—yet.

"You're nuts."

"You're welcome," he said with a grin.

Knowing for sure that Zach was straight didn't really change my world any, so I wasn't crushed with disappointment or anything. Fantasies aside, I knew I never had a chance with him, so his orientation didn't actually matter.

At practice, I was about twenty percent less nervous than I had been the first time. I had more of an idea what to expect, the coach didn't seem to regret asking me to join the team and even walking around mostly naked was less scary.

Of course, letting my guard down was a serious mistake.

As the guys horsed around while waiting for the coach to come out, I kept the same distance that I had before. I was watching Liam out of the corner of my eye and wondering what he looked for in a shot he chose to take.

My suit was suddenly yanked down below my ass.

The guys howled with laughter. I freaked out and reached down to yank it back up, cursing myself for forgetting the drawstring. I couldn't very well run and hide with my suit pulled down, after all.

But somewhere in the storm of panic and humiliation, I realized Liam was watching me and I didn't want to let him down. Isn't that nuts? I found myself wondering, "What would Liam do?" It was insane, because I was definitely not Liam. I didn't have his courage or his wit. But that part of me that has trouble with running when I should met up with his words about not living in fear and something inside me just sort of shifted.

I turned on Jimmy and made myself smile. Slowly and casually, I pulled my suit back up like I didn't really care. It was the best acting job of my life, since tears of humiliation were only being held back with willpower. Like Liam had said, though, if I couldn't be brave then I could fake it.

"If you wanted a look, sweetie, you could have just asked."

I was proud of myself for the little sneer I put on my face. And that I managed to not shake in terror.

The laughter stopped. A chorus of "Ooohs" rang out. Jimmy's smirk twisted into a furious glare—the ugliest expression I'd yet seen from him. I saw his hands curl into fists. This was no mere boyish banter. I had crossed a line. He was the alpha wolf and I, the stupid lone wolf with no sense, was challenging him in front of the whole pack.

~ 99 ~

As scary as it was, it also felt kind of amazing. It sure beat being scared all to pieces. Even if I did get my face broken for it, at least I hadn't looked like a scared little kid.

"Okay, boys, let's gather 'round, " Lancaster said, oblivious to the scene he had stumbled into. "Today we're going to work on the backstroke."

"Jimmy would rather work on a different stroke with his new boyfriend," Chad teased.

"Fuck you," Jimmy retorted, rounding on him.

Mayhem ensued. I rolled my eyes and got away from them, not wanting any part of it. So I think I was the only one who heard that at the end of the week, he would be deciding who stayed and who got cut. I found myself really hoping I made it, which surprised the hell out of me.

Bailey, who was a short, compact dude with brown curls, sidled over to me. "How many laps did Coach say?"

"Five," I replied.

He thanked me by way of a smile that showed his braces. I smiled back and got to my mark. The backstroke was a weird way to swim, but I did my best with it. The good thing was that I had to focus so hard on making my stupid arms and legs move in the right rhythm that I forgot all about Jimmy and the possibility he was plotting my death.

After practice, I was worn out. But it was a good worn out, the sort of worn out that reminded me I had done good. I thought maybe I could get used to that.

"Justin, can I talk to you a second?"

"Sure, coach," I said, wrapping my towel around my shoulders.

"I was wondering if you could hang around for a little bit? There's someone I want you to meet."

"Er, okay…."

"You're doing really good, Justin. With you and Jimmy, I think the Frosh-Soft team can do okay this year. But you're going to have to work."

"I thought I was."

Lancaster actually smiled. "You have, but it's going to take more to get you to where I know you can be. We've got just over a month to get you ready. You up for that, son?"

"I guess."

"Good. He'll be here in a few minutes, so just take a seat."

"Okay." I headed over to Liam, who questioned me with his eyes. "Coach wants me to meet somebody. Can you chill for a bit?"

"Sure." Liam gave me a proud look. "You really took that Jimmy down. It was priceless."

I blushed. "You liked?"

"Liked? I have it all on video! It'll get a million views on YouTube!"

"You what? Dude! That's so not cool! You can't—"

Liam laughed. "Kidding."

"Asshole," I griped, glaring at him.

"Aw, don't be a hater."

I rolled my eyes at him. "Jimmy's going to kick my ass."

"Or do something to it, anyway."

"Dude!" I hunkered down, embarrassed. "You're terrible."

"I'm just saying, the guy has a real thing for stripping other dudes."

"That makes him a jerk, not gay."

"Sorry to tell you, buddy, but a person can be both of those things."

I grumbled, not doubting that for a second. Lancaster called me over and as I came up to him my eyes fixed on the drop dead sexy dude standing next to him. I didn't know him, but I'd seen him in passing. He had bronze skin, the sort that you have to be born with because no amount of tanning will ever match it. His dark hair was buzzed short, like nearly down to the scalp. I supposed that made it easier to get the swim cap on and off. He was almost as tall as me, which was unusual. I'm used to looking downward when talking to people.

"Justin, this is Kanoa. He's on the varsity team."

"Hey," the gorgeous guy said.

I searched in vain for the vocabulary I'd been using my whole life. After an embarrassing several seconds, I managed to mumble something that combined "Hey" with "Hello" and then had a dash of "Hi" tacked onto it for added stupidity.

I am doomed to live a lonely, virginal life, I tell you.

"Kanoa is one of our best swimmers. I've asked him if he can help you out, and he said yes."

"Coach says you've got potential."

Of course he had a gorgeous smile; perfectly straight teeth, a slight upward quirk at the left corner, an adorable crinkling around his eyes. I looked into that radiant, friendly grin and lost all capacity for thought. I'm not kidding. My brain just totally shut down on me. I don't think I was even able to breathe.

"He does," Lancaster said. "I think he could be your successor."

"Oh, he's going to fill my suit when I'm gone?"

I almost passed out. "Huh?"

Kanoa looked down at his toes. "Sorry, that was gross. Not sure where that came from." He looked at me then with a sheepish smile. "Well, Justin, what do you say? You want to train with me?"

I nodded, since I didn't trust my vocal cords.

"Cool. Can you be at school at seven AM? That way we can use the pool and the weight room without interfering with classes. Bring your gym clothes."

I nodded again, my mind still blank. There was just too much flying at me. Coach thought I was that good? Kanoa was going to be my personal swimming instructor? I had to be at school at seven in the morning?

"Okay, well, I gotta go get the team into the weight room. See you tomorrow, Justin."

"Mm'k." That was all I managed, and it was kind of a squeak.

I was in a fog of delirium as I showered and changed. It was completely unbelievable and totally impossible, but I was actually happy. I'd joined a school team and I was happy. What was the world coming to?

CHAPTER 11

Liam wore a clean shirt to meet my mom. Either he wanted to impress her or he just wanted to be sure she didn't smell weed on him, I couldn't be sure. Of course, that didn't change the fact that he looked thuggish—I barely noticed anymore but my mom sure did. I could see from the way she sized Liam up that she doubted my taste in friends.

"I was going to order pizza for dinner, if you wanted to stay."

I hid a smile. My mom was kind of competitive. She wanted to prove she was as good a parent as Liam's folks. It was really nice of her, considering the way she kept sneaking disapproving glances at my new friend.

Liam's face lit up with joy. "Pizza? I am so there."

"What do you like on it?"

"Anything that's not good for me."

My mom's neutral mask cracked before the legendary Liam charm. I saw one corner of her lips twitch. "That's pretty much everything."

"Sounds delicious."

Once I got Liam alone in my room, though, I had to be the bad guy. "Is this okay, though? Your mom keeps you on a pretty strict diet."

Liam wrinkled his nose at me. "Traitor."

"Sorry, dude."

"I eat all the healthy, macro-biotic rabbit food she gives me. A few slices of pizza won't kill me."

"Okay."

"But, uh, you can't tell her, okay? We have to keep this on the DL."

I laughed and flopped on my bed. "Okay."

"So, who was the dude your coach introduced you to?"

I felt warm all over. A stupid grin took over my face that I couldn't seem to stop. "Kanoa. He's a varsity swimmer. Coach asked him to help me train."

"I think someone has a new crush," Liam remarked, smirking that smirk of his.

"Shut up," I told him, throwing a pillow at him.

Liam threw it right back at me. "Poor Zach. Well, you snooze, you lose. He had his chance to ride the Justin train all the way to the station."

"Oh my God," I whined, hiding my face in the pillow. "You are so awful."

Liam laughed. "Zach, Jimmy, now Kanoa. What do you put in that milkshake of yours that brings all the boys to the yard?"

I glowered over the edge of the pillow. "Secret ingredients."

Liam snickered. "So, it's like that? Not even a little hint for the loveless?"

"Nope. We gays don't share our tricks."

"That sucks."

"That's just *one* of our secrets."

He burst out laughing. "*Now* who's being awful?"

I picked at a loose thread in the pillow. "He's so hot," I breathed. "Like, seriously. That smile could blind a guy. And his eyes? Oh man…. And there's this divot in his chin…. " I gave Liam a hard look. "And no, I'm not asking him out."

"Does the wing man have to step in again?"

"Don't you dare."

We listened to music and ate pizza and generally had a good time. His mom picked him up and there was that weird moment when parents meet. My mom looked shocked to see that his mother looked so normal. I doubted Anna could pick up on that, but I knew my mom really well. I could see what she was thinking like it was written on her face.

Anna was very friendly. She didn't even make a fuss about the pizza box that was clearly on the kitchen table. I supposed Liam would hear about it later, though.

After they left, my mom cut off my escape to my room and sat me down. "Anna seems nice."

There was a silent, "Not sure how she could have a boy like Liam" at the end of her statement that annoyed me. Sure, I'd treated him like he was a stoner loser at first, but now that I saw past that I didn't like anyone else judging him by his looks.

"Liam's cool."

My mom sighed. "I know boys like him seem really interesting, but they're bad news."

I folded my arms. "You don't know him."

"I just…. Why can't you make friends with someone else? You're on the swim team now."

"Mom," I told her, snapping. "Liam's the reason I'm on the team. He's a great guy."

"Does he do drugs?"

"Mom!"

"Does he?"

"No," I lied. Well, it was only sort of a lie. Pot was more like medicine for him. "You should give him a chance."

My mom gave me a long, hard stare like she knew I was keeping something from her. "You're just doing so well now. I don't want this boy messing all that up for you."

I glowered at her, resenting her for refusing to listen to me. After a second, I got up and stormed off to my room and slammed the door behind me.

Parents! I thought.

I got online in the hopes of finding Hawaii to vent at. He knew all about parents and their frustrating habit of expecting you to act like an adult while treating you like a kid. He had told me about his parents and how they seemed to have his whole life planned out.

Sadly for me, Hawaii wasn't on. For a while, I just stared at my screen. My screen saver image was the picture Liam had taken of me. I know that makes me sound seriously vain, but the picture just amazed me. I could hardly believe it was me. I certainly didn't fit the title of the picture at all. I was about as far from "fearless" as one could get.

Liam had so much talent, no matter what he thought. The picture on my screen should be hanging in a gallery somewhere.

"It really should," I thought, inspiration hitting me.

I started looking for online amateur photo contests. They weren't hard to find, but it took a while to read through all the rules before I found one that seemed the right fit. It specifically targeted young up-and-coming photographers. I looked at the previous year's winner and I was sure Liam was better.

I filled out the form and printed it. I used Liam's name but my address—that way, if he lost, he'd never have to know about it. The picture would need to be printed, but my old inkjet was not up to the task. I decided I'd do it at the local office supply place tomorrow after my practice with Kanoa.

As far as that goes, I was so excited about spending time with Kanoa that I didn't even mind getting up early for school. Of course, I had no idea what I'd actually agreed to. It didn't matter, though. It could have been running naked through some rose bushes and I would have gone along with it just to be around Kanoa.

"Morning!" he greeted me with far more cheeriness than anyone should have at seven AM.

I managed a smile. "Hi." At least I was up to single syllables now. I take what victories I can.

"We're going to run some laps first. It's a good way to wake up in the morning."

I firmly disagreed with that statement. Running, I felt, was something that should be reserved for when you had a machete-wielding lunatic in a hockey mask chasing you. I didn't argue, though. There wasn't any point. I was in his hands now.

Somewhere on the second lap, I managed to trip over my own feet and went sprawling. I was furious with myself and humiliated. I wished again for the power to laugh at myself so that I could make some joke to make the whole stupid incident less degrading. All I could think of, though, was how I had just made a fool of myself in front of the guy I was crushing on.

"Guess you're more of a fish than a gazelle," Kanoa said as he helped me up.

I brushed myself off. "There was a rock," I lied, feeling even more stupid.

Kanoa didn't laugh or call me a liar. "You okay?"

My pride is broken, but there's no bandage for that. "Yeah."

"Come on, two more laps and then we'll hit the weights."

I almost refused, but he was already moving and I didn't know what to do other than follow along—but now I was much more mindful of my feet.

My embarrassment got worse when we got to the weight room. I was barely able to manage half the weight he exercised with. But my stupid pride pushed me to take on more than I wanted. What made it even stupider was that I was trying to impress him.

"Dude, less is more," he told me as he lowered the weight I was doing.

"No, I can handle it."

"Too much muscle slows you down, so you want more tone than mass," he instructed. "You got to trust me."

I felt so totally lame. "Sorry."

"Dude, none of us are born athletes. I was skinnier than you when I was a freshman."

"No way."

"Seriously."

I still felt lame, but I made myself stick with his instructions. It wore me out, and by the time we were done I felt like my limbs were all made of rubber. I've heard people talk about some sort of high they get from exercising, but I just felt awful.

Even as I was wondering if I really had it in me to keep up this additional training, Kanoa told me I did a great job and flashed me a smile and I forgot all about my aching body.

I rode that high all the way to fourth period, where a storm was brewing. Zach did not give me that great big grin of his. He did not ask me how anything was hanging. He barely offered me a "hi" as I sat down. Figuring something had happened that was none of my business, I just got out my textbook and tried to finish the reading I was behind on.

"Is that Liam guy a friend of yours?"

I froze. I'd forgotten about Liam's idiotic but well-meaning chat with Zach. "Yeah."

Zach nodded, doodling in his notebook. "Thought so."

I almost asked why, but then I stopped myself because there was really no answer to that question that wouldn't lead somewhere bad. My shoulders tensed as I hunched over my textbook. But try as I might, I couldn't keep my eyes from sliding sideways to look at him.

Zach's doodle was a nonsensical swirl as his pencil circled around and around. I'd never seen him look so unhappy. My stomach churned.

"I just don't know why you would think…. I don't know how I came off as…."

Zach was never going to be the world's best thinker, but he'd put it together. It wasn't like Liam was spotted on campus with a lot of different people. So who else could this mysterious gay friend of his be?

"I didn't," I told Zach. "Not at all. Liam was just checking because…. I don't know. He just was. I'm sorry."

Zach broke the lead on his pencil. "Okay."

It didn't sound okay, but there wasn't anything I could do. Zach was uncomfortable around me now and I couldn't fix it. Liam was to blame and by all rights I should have been pissed at him, but instead I was mad at Zach. I'd never once hit on him. Why was he acting like such a big baby just because I was interested—or used to be interested—in him?

Was I really so repulsive that my being attracted to him was that offensive?

The death of my crush on Zach was a painful event that took the entire uncomfortable class period. By the end, I was ready to ask for a different lab partner, but I doubted anyone would be willing to trade—not to be stuck with me. So there was nothing I could do about it.

It's just really hard when your heroes disappoint you.

CHAPTER 12

When I'd agreed to train with Kanoa, I didn't realize how hard it would be to deal with two practices a day. It pushed me to my limits, which was awful. But then I noticed how those limits expanded, and that felt really good. And of course I lived for those little moments of praise from Kanoa.

Monday, Wednesday and Friday were jogging around the track and laps in the pool. Tuesday and Thursday were more jogging and weight training. It was brutal, but all he had to do was smile at me and I'd find the reserves somewhere in me to do one more lap, one more rep.

"You're already fast, we're just making you faster," he told me one morning.

It helped, though. Like I said, I've never been an athlete, so I had zero knowledge of how to get in shape.

The various machines in the weight room were like bizarre, scary Medieval torture devices. I had no idea where to even start, but Kanoa walked me through them and showed me the best routine.

So for once, I was ahead of the curve when the rest of my team was brought into the weight room for the first time. While Jimmy worked on impressing everyone with how much weight he could lift, I took my place at another machine and did the reps Kanoa had assigned me.

"Can I partner up with you?" Bailey asked.

The last time anyone had asked to partner with me on anything had been kindergarten and that had only been because I'd hoarded all the red crayons. I stared up at him in disbelief. My surprise only deepened when I saw him looking nervous, like he was expecting me to tell him to piss off.

I remembered what Liam had told me; how people thought I was stuck up. I still didn't understand that, but I wasn't going to let that label stick.

"Sure," I told Bailey and showed him the routine.

I noticed as we worked out that more of the guys were paying attention to me. At first I thought it was because they were snickering about how weak I was. But then I noticed more of them dropping the weight they were doing so they could do more reps. They were following my lead, which was a shock since I didn't know I *had* a "lead."

Lancaster was nowhere to be found. He'd said he had to make a phone call and left us. I'd expected him to come in and correct Jimmy and his pack of idiots. But that wasn't happening. When it came to supervision, apparently the coach had a strict hands-off policy.

"We want to build tone," I told Bailey, but letting my voice carry. "Bulking up will slow us down."

"Some of us can use some bulk, matchstick," Jimmy sneered.

I ignored him. He didn't matter. What mattered was that way more people were paying attention to me than I liked. As in, just about everyone was eying me. Being the center of attention was something I tried really hard to avoid. But there I was, with everyone looking at me like they were waiting for me to drop more pearls of wisdom.

"Kanoa told me—"

"You're friends with Kanoa?" Jon asked, looking really impressed. "That guy's a legend."

"Er, I'm training with him."

I meant it to be a clarification, a way of making sure I wasn't claiming friendship status with a school demigod. Only, once the words were out of my mouth, I realized they sounded like bragging. I sort of thought that was worse.

Of course, the thing is, I was surrounded by guys. Guys love bragging. It's like the natural dialect—I'd just never spoken it before. So I got a lot of grins and impressed looks and a whole room full of something I think was respect—I couldn't be sure, since it had been so long since I'd seen any.

"Okay, so, he showed me some routines he uses—"

"Can you show us?"

"Uh…."

"Come on, dude, why should Maui be the only one you help out?" Chad asked.

I glanced at Bailey, wondering about the nickname. He surprised me by blushing and looking down at his sneakers. I'd ask later, I decided.

I didn't need to look at Jimmy to know that the alpha wolf was pissed again. And, well, I didn't care. I don't know if it makes me an asshole, but I really liked all this new respect. I'd never felt anything like it.

"Okay, Tony, your posture is all wrong. You're taking too much weight with your back...."

Yeah, it was pretty cool. Even the murderous looks from Jimmy didn't bother me. Mostly, it was because I knew he no longer had the whole team under his spell. He could hate me, but he couldn't bully me anymore.

But the best part was watching him, sullenly and quietly, copying the routines I was showing to the guys. I knew that had to burn up his guts, and that made it all the sweeter. I never claimed to be a saint. That sounds boring anyway.

"Maui?" I asked Bailey as we all headed for the locker room.

"It's a nickname I got in middle school," he explained, looking annoyed. "Chad was in my gym class, so he remembers."

"Are you from Hawaii?"

Bailey's fair cheeks colored again. "No, I have a birthmark that looks like an island."

"I never saw—"

"It's in a place most people don't usually see."

I couldn't help but smile. "That's great. I wish I had a cool nickname."

Bailey was still blushing. "It's not that cool."

He did offer me a faint little smile, though.

Friday came and even though I was feeling confident (for the first time in the history of ever) I still went to my locker after practice with the faintest bit of dread churning in my stomach. Two guys were going to find a pink card in their locker, telling them they were off the team.

What may shock you to find out is that I actually didn't want Jimmy to be one of them. He was really good and certainly the best athlete we had. And, well, he made great décor for the locker room, if you know what I'm saying. I was sure I could deal with his BS, and I wanted my team to do well.

My team…. That was such a weird thought. I sucked at teams. Every time I found myself on a team, I was the one they hated, the one they wanted to bury in a shallow grave. But I was fitting in, making a place for myself.

I didn't want to give it up.

But I didn't have to. Two guys, Ray and Greg, got the boot. I wasn't really surprised. They didn't goof around like Jimmy, but they only ever put in the bare minimum effort. Neither of them seemed to care about being cut, either, so I guess it wasn't a tragedy.

Afternoons with Liam were still the best part of my day, though. He loved to hear all about the stuff with the team. His excitement and interest made it even better. When I told him I made the cut, he let out an adorable whoop of delight before saying that he had known all along I'd make it.

"Does your mom have any recipe books I can borrow?" I asked Liam one Saturday as we walked Sully to the park.

"Why, do you have someone you need to poison?"

I laughed. "Dude, your mom is a great cook."

"You take that back right now."

I shook my head. "Kanoa has been telling me I have to eat better stuff."

"Oh, I see."

He said it in this sing-song voice he liked to use when he was trying to find some way to make something innocent into something dirty.

"My mom is always working, so she doesn't have time to cook. I was thinking maybe I could learn how."

Liam's grin dimmed a little bit. I didn't like the tinge of sadness there at all. It was way too much like pity. I didn't want anyone feeling sorry for me.

"You can eat over whenever you want."

I blushed and looked down. "I appreciate that. And that's cool. But I would like to see if I can make some of those things your mom makes. It would be nice if my mom ate better too."

"Okay, I'll ask her. But I won't ever forgive you. Your house was the only junk food refuge I had left. Even my dad won't hook me up anymore."

That evening Anna showed me how to make food without burning the house down or causing the health department to invade with haz-mat suits. I was amazed there wasn't any magic to it, just measuring and mixing. I decided to surprise my mom by making her dinner. She worked so hard, I figured it would be a nice thing for her to come home to.

It was kind of fun, too. I put on my tunes and sang along and did my stupid dance moves while I heated and boiled and mixed. Everything went together fine and it smelled great. I was happy, anticipating the stunned look on my mom's face when she walked in.

So imagine my surprise when she came home and looked bothered. She poked her nose into the oven and then looked over the range and the pots boiling and then gave me the weirdest look I'd ever seen on her face. Like I say, I can usually guess what she's thinking, but this look was new. Her brow was furrowed and her face was pinched, but there was worry in her eyes.

"If you wanted me to cook something, hon, you could have asked."

"I thought I'd surprise you." Now I was frowning. What the hell was going on?

She hung her purse on a peg, not speaking to me for a moment. "I'm sorry we've been eating so much take-out."

"Mom, will you relax?" She made to take over the stove, but I swiped the spoon before she could reach it. "What's wrong?"

"It's just not appropriate, kiddo. Mothers cook for their family, not sons."

I stared at her. "Are you kidding me?"

"Why don't you let me finish up here? Go set the table."

This was not going as planned, not at all. "Why can't I do something nice for you?"

"I appreciate the thought, kiddo. I just wish you'd talked to me first."

"Why?"

I think she meant her smile to be kind, but it just seemed condescending. "It's a nice gesture, hon, but people might get the wrong impression."

"What impression?"

She nodded to the apron I was wearing. "That you're, you know, one of *those* men."

"Straight men cook, mom."

She shook her head, dismissing that idea out of hand. Sometimes I forget that my mom grew up in a very conservative family. It was easy to forget, since we never saw that side of the family and she almost never talked about them.

"I'm just saying, you could give people the wrong idea."

I was pissed. Here I'd been expecting her to be thrilled and grateful and instead she was acting like I had violated some sacred gender code. The idea that even the appearance of being gay was so bothersome to her that she couldn't just enjoy the surprise dinner I'd made her had me gnashing my teeth.

"Maybe it's not the wrong idea."

She gave me a blank look. "What are you talking about?"

"I'm gay."

The words just slipped out. I was hurt and angry and it was the first thing I could think of to lash out with.

The blood drained from her face. "That's not true."

The noodles boiled over, hissing all over the ceramic range top. "It is true." I felt so cold inside, so horribly, terribly cold.

"You're not gay."

"Yes I am!" I knew I sounded like a five-year-old, but I didn't care.

My mom's eyed filled with tears. "Why would you say that? Who made you think that? Was it that Liam boy? I knew he was trouble."

"Mom, no one *made* me gay."

"Is this about me divorcing your father?"

I wanted to scream, laugh and cry all at the same time. "Mom, I was born this way."

"That's a lie. Someone's been filling your head with lies."

I felt tears clawing their way out of me, but I battled them back. *Don't you fucking dare start crying*, I told myself. *Don't you fucking dare.*

"Mom, this is who I am. I'm still your son. I'm still the same guy."

She started to cry, softly and quietly. "We'll get you help. We'll fix this."

"I'm not broken," I told her. "I'm just gay."

She sobbed harder. It was like every time I said I was gay it was a slap in her face. I couldn't take it. I just couldn't. I went into my room and grabbed my backpack. I stuffed some clothes into it and then headed for the front door.

"Where do you think you're going?"

"What do you care?" I said and stormed out.

By the time I was down the stairs, I was shaking all over. At the end of the block, I couldn't seem to breathe. I made it to a bus stop and collapsed onto the bench. But I didn't cry. I would *not* allow myself to do that. I wasn't a little kid. I wasn't weak. I could and would fucking cope.

When I managed to calm down a little, I got out my phone and called Liam. "Can I crash on your couch?" My voice sounded shaky and I couldn't seem to make it stop.

"Justin? What happened?"

I tried to explain, but the words just crashed into each other and I made a total mess of it. I didn't want to make my mom sound like the villain, so I stammered and stumbled through the explanation, making little to no sense.

"Where are you?" he finally asked.

I told him the cross-streets. "I can catch a bus."

"Stay where you are. I'll be there in a bit."

"Okay."

By the time Liam arrived, driven by his mom, I was pretty much a wreck. I felt awful for making my mom cry. I felt awful because I couldn't handle it on my own. And I felt really awful for making Liam drag his mom out of the house to deal with my drama.

But when Liam grabbed me and pulled me into a hug, I just sagged against him.

"You've had a tough night, huh?"

I snorted laughter, but it sounded manic and crazed to my ears. "Never a dull moment."

He got me into the car. I guess he'd managed to work out what had happened from my disjointed blathering on the phone and told his mom, because Anna didn't ask me why I looked like a patient who had escaped from the asylum.

"Does your mother know where you are?" was all she asked.

I shook my head. "Don't think she cares."

That made Anna's face crease with unhappiness. "I'm sure she does. You can stay the night, Justin, but we have to let her know where you are."

"Okay."

I was just so grateful to have somewhere to go that I didn't argue. Anna took care of everything, calling my mom and dealing with all the drama there. I didn't bother listening in. I just went with Liam to his room and sat with him on his bed and stared blankly ahead for the longest time.

Liam kept his arm around my shoulders, which was great and stupid all at the same time. I mean, it made me feel better, but knowing his situation made my problems seem trivial. Sure, my mom was disgusted by me, but at least I didn't have a life-threatening illness.

Liam, of course, didn't point out how dumb I was being. He was too kind-hearted.

"What made you tell her?" he asked after what seemed like forever.

"Sudden onset stupidity," I said, looking down at my hands.

"You're not the one to blame here, dude," Liam insisted. "You're who you are and she has to learn to deal."

I shook my head. "You should have seen her face. She'll never accept it."

"Well, we'll see."

I swallowed against the lump in my throat. "I knew it would go this way. But, you know, I think there was this stupid part of me that thought that maybe she would be okay with it. Like, I don't know, that maybe she would love me more than she hates my orientation."

"Your mom will come around."

I hoped he was right. I didn't know what I would do otherwise. I couldn't move into Liam's house—they had no room and couldn't take on another mouth to feed. I certainly wasn't going to go to my dad.

Without any answers, I curled up on Liam's floor and went to sleep, hoping that I would wake up to the realization that this had all been a terrible nightmare.

CHAPTER 13

I slept very badly, tossing and turning and fleeing from one terrible dream to another. I finally gave it up altogether as the sun began to rise. I grabbed my bag and quietly slipped out, careful to not disturb Liam.

I was groggy and out of sorts as I changed into my gym clothes, wrestling with the problem I'd created for myself. I couldn't believe how stupid I had been. My mouth was always getting me into trouble, and now it had really screwed me over. Why couldn't I ever learn to just shut up?

Why did I always fail at everything?

"Whoa, you look terrible," Kanoa said when he came in

"Thanks," I replied, glowering at my toes.

His smile faded at my tone. "Sorry, I didn't mean.... I was just.... Ah, shit, dude, I was just being stupid."

I shook my head, not wanting to take my mood out on him. "No, I was being an ass."

Kanoa looked worried now. "What's wrong?"

"Nothing."

"Doesn't seem like nothing."

I wasn't sure why he cared. He was acting like we were friends. I wanted that to be true, but I'd gotten into trouble before by assuming things like that. I decided to proceed with caution and just give him a quick answer. That way, if he was just being nice, he could quickly move on.

"I had a fight with my mom last night."

"Looks like it was a doozy. Care to talk about it?"

I was so exhausted, physically and emotionally, I almost teared up at this little offer of sympathy from a guy who had no reason to care about any of my bullshit. "It's okay."

"You know what? Screw practice. I skipped breakfast. Let's go get waffles. My treat."

I firmly stomped on any compulsion to sniffle. "That.... That would be really nice."

My emotions were all over the place and my head was a mess, but I had enough sense to skip some details about the fight with my mom. After Zach and then my mom's reactions, I just couldn't bear the idea of Kanoa looking at me like I had a disease. So I just made up a story about how my mom didn't think I was contributing enough around the house.

Kanoa didn't look like he bought it, but he didn't push it either. Instead, we talked about swimming and who we thought were the best on our teams. We talked about school and our best and worst subjects. I wouldn't be able to tell you what all was said. I just remember the warm feeling of friendship and the way it made everything seem less bleak.

I just wished I didn't have to lie to people to keep them from hating me.

Liam looked very worried about me when he met me in English class. "Why didn't you wake me?"

I shrugged. "I had to get to practice. And you were so adorable drooling into your pillow."

"I don't drool," he argued. He eyed me, trying to see if my wan smile was some sort of mask, I guess. "How are you holding up?"

"I'm fine," I lied. "I found this great cardboard box with a fantastic alley view. I'm going to move in after school."

"Not funny."

"Damn, I worked on that one all morning."

"Justin—"

"Liam, can we not? Please? I'm trying to not fall apart here."

He looked even more worried. "Okay."

I tried to put my problems out of my mind, but they loomed like a thundercloud over everything. I couldn't escape them. School, the team, friends, none of it was going to be right until I fixed things at home. I had to face off with my mom again.

I spent the whole day trying to figure out what I would say. I considered everything, including total surrender and promising my mom I would repent my evil homosexual lifestyle. It wasn't like I was going to be doing anything gay anytime soon, apart from listening to Lady Gaga. But I resented the idea of having to lie like that. Really, no option seemed appealing, and by the time I got home, I still had no plan.

My mom was waiting for me. She sat at the kitchen table, going through bills. I stopped just inside the door and watched her, waiting for her to speak. I figured she would tear into me about running out, or yell at me for going to Liam. But she just sat there, silently, like I was invisible. Maybe I just didn't exist for her anymore.

"Mom…."

"I spoke to your father," she said, still not looking at me. "We agreed you should go live with him for a while."

A dozen emotions roiled in my stomach. I went with anger. "Oh, you and he decided? Thanks for asking what I thought."

"We're your parents, kiddo. This isn't a democracy."

"So, you don't want me around?"

"That's not it at all," she said crisply. "But you've been hanging around with a bad element who is putting these ideas into your head."

"Like thinking for myself and looking out for what I want?"

She ignored me. "I just think it would be better for you to spend time with your father."

"Yeah, he's a much better influence," I said, my lip curling. "I want to learn how to treat a woman like crap just like him."

"Justin, that's enough."

"Mom…." I let my anger go, expelling it with a sigh. It was wearing me out, holding onto it. "I'm not going to go live with Dad. If you can't handle having a gay son, I'll go live somewhere else. But I've got friends, now, a team, a life. I won't give that up."

She slammed her hand down on the table and glared at me. "Justin, I don't know where this attitude is coming from but I've had all I can take."

"Okay then," I said, clamping down on a torrent of sadness and hurt. "I'll be back for my stuff."

I was halfway through the door when she called my name. I stopped, wanting her to say something to walk us back from this cliff we were at. I think she sensed, just like I did, that if I walked out the door, she'd lose me forever. I didn't want that to happen. I hoped she didn't either.

"You'd rather live with that boy than your family?"

"That 'boy' is my best friend," I told her. "And *he* doesn't care that I'm gay."

"Is that the life you want? Drugs and that whole … *lifestyle* with him?"

"Wait…." I turned. "You don't think Liam's my boyfriend, do you?"

The word clearly repulsed her. "You weren't like this before you met him."

"Yes, I was. I just didn't tell you."

I sighed and closed the door and went to sit across from her. Liam didn't like people knowing about his disease because he didn't like people treating him different. I respected that, so I never told anyone what I knew. But this time I was going to make an exception. I hoped he wouldn't mind.

"Liam's not gay, mom. He's got leukemia. The only drugs he does are the ones he needs to stay alive."

She stared at me. It was amazing to watch her face transform from embittered disappointment to sympathetic understanding. "Why didn't you tell me?"

"He doesn't want people to know."

My mom looked away, processing this piece of information. It totally derailed the train of righteous indignation she had been riding.

I still couldn't believe she'd thought Liam had turned me gay. Where did she get her information from, anyway?

"He seems healthy."

I shrugged. "He is, mostly."

She turned back to me, looking at me like she was trying to find the little boy she'd raised somewhere in my face. I kind of felt sorry for her, in that moment. She didn't want me to be gay. She wanted me to have the life she'd imagined for me when I'd been that little boy.

"Do you have homework?" she asked.

"Some."

"Why don't you go do that while I pay bills? Then we can go get some Italian."

I felt my heart pounding against my ribs. "Mom…."

"I don't understand this, Justin. And it's not what I want for you. But I don't want you to run away, either. You're my son and I love you. We'll just have to figure it out."

It wasn't what I wanted, but it was all I was going to get. I got up and grabbed my backpack and headed for my room. I called Liam to let him know things were leveling out, if not improving.

"That's good to hear. Just give her time," Liam advised.

I did feel worlds better, though. Even if my mom didn't like the fact that I was gay, she was at least trying to cope with it. It was the "trying" part that made all the difference. The complete rejection she'd started with had been too much to handle. The situation wasn't at all comfortable—dinner was an awkward affair that night—

but at least the secret was out and I didn't have it
hanging over me anymore.

CHAPTER 14

I was in a much better mood when I showed up for training the next morning. I'd gotten some real sleep, which helped. With things at home less scary, I was able to focus on the fact that Kanoa had been so incredibly kind to me the day before. Training with him was already fantastic, but the idea that we were becoming friends made it so much better. I was even thinking of asking him on another waffle friend-date—just to say thank you.

I got quite an unwelcome surprise when I spotted Kanoa talking to some girl I'd never seen or heard of before. I stopped out of earshot, not wanting to eavesdrop. They seemed to be arguing. They used a lot of very big hand gestures. And then there was hugging. I didn't like the hugging *at all*.

Of course he has a girlfriend, you idiot.

I'd even sort of assumed there was some girlfriend-person somewhere. But having her show up during *my time* with Kanoa filled me with this overpowering jealousy. Couldn't she leave me the space to have my fantasies? Was that so much to ask?

When she departed, I approached him, forcing the sour look off my face. "Morning."

He beamed at me. "You look better."

"Yeah, I sort of worked things out with my mom."

"Oh good. Congrats."

"Thanks." I wanted to tell him how much it meant to me that he'd taken the time to look out for me yesterday. But that just sounded weird in my head. Instead, I said, "Guess we should work off those waffles."

At least that got a grin from him. "So, three weeks from the first meet. You excited?"

I was terrified, but I didn't want to show that. "Can't wait."

"You're doing the one-hundred meter freestyle?"

"That's what Lancaster told me."

"That's my race."

"Any advice?"

"Be faster than the other guys."

I laughed. "Thanks a lot."

His responding laugh was like music in my ears. Oh yeah, I was in serious crush land.

Things at home remained tense, but there wasn't anything to do about it. Spending time with Liam made it a lot easier to bear. Whoever said laughter is the best medicine was one smart person.

Zach did end up asking for a new partner. My new table-mate was a girl named Shelly who spent the whole class texting. That was fine with me. I was just glad to not have Zach and his unpleasant homophobia sitting next to me. I had too many other things on my mind, like a swim meet that was coming up pretty fast.

Most of the team was buckling down and getting ready. Jimmy, of course, kept up his pranks because he's apparently a five-year-old in a teenager's body. I kept expecting the coach to say something to him, but Lancaster seemed way too willing to let the team sort out its own problems.

As I came out of the locker room one day, I came on this really twisted scene. Jimmy, who really needed to fucking grow up already, had invented a new game. Somehow, he and his jerk friends had gotten Bailey's suit off of him and were playing keep away with it.

I barely had time to wonder where the coach was before I charged in.

Bailey was holding up better than I would in the situation. He had one hand over his bits while with the other he was trying to get his suit back. I would have bolted for the locker room if had been me. Either Bailey was incredibly brave or he was so freaked out the idea hadn't yet occurred to him.

One advantage of being six feet tall? Keep away is a game you always win. I grabbed the suit in midair and handed it to Bailey. Then I turned on Jimmy, ready to fight for the first time in my life. I was just totally pissed. I'd had it with his bullshit.

"What the fuck is wrong with you?"

Jimmy rolled his eyes. "We're just having some fun, matchstick."

"Bailey's on your team, you dumb fuck."

Fearless

Everyone stared at me. Even Bailey just stood there, his suit in one hand, his eyes wide in absolute astonishment. No one could believe what they were seeing.

The air crackled with tension as the alpha wolf and his challenger faced off once again before the pack. This would be the last time, though, I decided.

"You think you're something?" Jimmy sneered. "You think you're all that? The coach only asked you to be on the team because he felt sorry for you. I heard him say it."

It was a really good, really low blow. A couple of weeks ago, it would have crippled me. But things had changed.

"I don't think I'm all anything," I said, surprised by my calm. After facing off with my mom, though, this just didn't seem that scary. "I'm just here to swim. But we're a team, not your personal toys to fuck with. I don't know *what* your fucking little psychodrama is. I don't know if you're queer and taking it out on everyone around you or just an asshole. But knock it off."

"Did you just call me a fag?" Jimmy asked, his voice low and dangerous.

"No, I just said you might be queer the way you like yanking guys' suits off."

That was the breaking point. Jimmy's handsome face contorted into something ugly and scary and he came at me. It was just him, though. He'd lost all of his fans and all of his support. He needed to put me down if he was going to get his alpha status back.

The Flying Spaghetti Monster or whoever is up there has a sense of humor, though. Because just before he reached me, he slipped on the wet cement, flailed and went into the pool. The whole team laughed, because it was the worst end of a bully in the history of the world.

But then I noticed he wasn't coming back up.

"He's faking it," Chad said.

"Too scared to surface," Tony said.

I'm the current expert on falls though. I know what a real fall looks like, and I know that when you're in one, you don't have any control. It's pretty easy to knock your head onto something. I dove into the pool, straight down to where Jimmy was blissfully sinking.

He was a limp rag when I grabbed a hold of him (from behind, like we're taught). I pushed off the bottom and brought us to the surface. Jimmy didn't stir, which freaked me out. The rest of the team stopped laughing when they saw it. Bailey, Chad and Tony all leaped in to help me.

We got Jimmy out and onto the concrete. Fortunately, Bailey knew CPR, so he took over. I sat back and waited, quietly freaking out about having accidentally killed a teammate. That was a new level of fail for me. And I'd thought I'd gone as low as I could.

But Jimmy sputtered and coughed up pool water a few seconds later. Everyone let out a cheer and Bailey got a lot of pats on the back.

"What the hell is going on out here?"

We all turned to the coach, a chorus of innocent faces. "Nothing," I said.

"Jimmy slipped and hit his head is all," Chad added.

"I told you all to stop horsing around. Someone take Jimmy to the nurse."

"I'll do it," Kent volunteered.

Jimmy was in bad shape as he wobbled to his feet. He leaned heavily on Kent, groaning a little from the massive headache he had. I hoped it would teach him a lesson.

"Thanks," Bailey whispered to me. "I owe you one."

I was still riding an adrenaline high. I could feel it coursing through me, making my fingers and toes tingle. "Don't mention it," I told him with a grin. "How was kissing Jimmy?"

Bailey went beet-red. "Like kissing day-old trout."

The face-off with Jimmy elevated me in the team's eyes, which was flattering. Some of them actually *talked* to me. And Jon high-fived me after I beat him in the fifty-meter freestyle. I still had no earthly idea what to say or do to come off as cool, but they seemed to accept me anyway.

CHAPTER 15

As October faded away, day by day, I got more and more anxious. This translated into me practicing even harder every day. I knew I had no hope of winning, but if I could somehow get third place then all of the coach's faith and Kanoa's time would not seem so wasted.

For once in my life, I just didn't want to fail completely. Was that too lofty a goal?

Those heavy worries were compounded by something really unexpected. Because, really, what I needed was something *else* to stress about.

"Gather round," Lancaster ordered one day before practice.

I was expecting another of his motivational speeches. I mean, they were cool and all but I was anxious to get into the water. I was determined to shave another second off my time.

"It's time for you guys to elect a team captain," Lancaster said. "Obviously, since you all have your individual races, this isn't someone to be in charge of the team. It's really just someone you can call if you can't reach me when you're sick or going to be late or your Aunt Dinah is in the hospital."

Everyone looked around and murmured while I chewed my thumbnail. I didn't care who the team captain was. I expected it would be Jimmy, because he was popular and voting always goes to the most popular person. And that was fine. Like Lancaster said, it wasn't like the captain was really in charge of anything.

I was more concerned with the problem of figuring out how I could get in more time in the weight room and the pool between now and the first swim meet. I was even considering asking if I could be at school at six AM, so you know I was freaking out.

"It's got to be Justin."

"Huh?" I asked, looking over at Jimmy.

He was giving me a weird smile. Okay, it was a friendly smile, but it was weird because it was coming from him. We hadn't spoken since that day he'd nearly drowned. I hadn't expected a thank you, not from him. And I hadn't really needed one, either. It was enough that he had been less of an ass since that incident.

To my absolute shock, the other guys started to nod their heads. Bailey gave me a grin and said, "Makes sense to me."

"Uh, wait a second." I wasn't really sure why I was objecting. I just didn't think I could handle any more responsibility right then.

"All in favor?" Jimmy asked.

Everyone but me raised their hands. And that was that. I had been drafted. I mean, yes, it was sort of flattering. How couldn't I be a little buzzed? Like I said, these things are popularity contests, so it was hard to ignore that the vote meant people sort of liked me.

Of course, that will all change when I lose at the first meet.

And that was what really made me sick with stress. Now I was some sort of leader, the guy the team looked to in some way. My failure (which was inevitable) was going to be so very much worse to bear.

I was having such a good time on the team and feeling like I had finally found my place that even the thought of having it all go to shit when I lost just killed me inside.

I had nightmares about it. In one, I would jump into the pool and find my suit missing, then see Jimmy had it and I would chase him around the pool while the other swimmers did their laps. In another, I was in class when Ms. Warner asked me why I wasn't at the meet that had started a half hour before. My subconscious had all sorts of scenarios in which I failed spectacularly.

I was involved in one of those nocturnal disturbances when I was awakened by a hand over my mouth.

As a way of waking up, I don't recommend it.

I struggled, but there were other hands holding my wrists. In fact, there were way more hands on me than I cared for. They hauled me out of bed and then put a blindfold on me. Shaken from sleep, I was too groggy to put up much of a fight.

"Welcome to the team."

It was Kanoa's voice. I relaxed. He'd warned me that some sort of initiation was going to happen soon, but he'd refused to tell me when or what. I couldn't figure out how they'd coordinated everything, but that confusion had to be put aside as they dragged me out my apartment.

I was glad I was in my sleep shorts as opposed to just my briefs like I sometimes will do.

I was deposited in an SUV like some sort of hostage in a movie. Knowing that it was Kanoa and the varsity guys made it a fun little adventure. I wondered what the initiation would be like. The only examples I had of such things came from some very, well, explicit videos. I doubted very much that the night was going in that direction.

Not that I would have minded all that much. Not if Kanoa was involved.

When the SUV stopped, I found myself deposited on sand-covered asphalt. That and the salty air told me we'd gone to the beach. I shivered against the crisp night air but I didn't complain. I wasn't going to embarrass myself in front of Kanoa.

I heard murmurs around me. I guessed it was the rest of the new guys on the team. I could have taken off the blindfold, but I didn't think that was part of the game. So I just waited in darkness, feeling goose-bumps break out on my arms from both excitement and serious cold.

We were marched down towards the water, which was a nightmare for me. The sand shifting under my feet made the footing treacherous. It would be really easy to trip, even if I could see. Not having my eyes made it so much worse. I paid very close attention to my steps, threatening my feet with amputation if they betrayed me.

At last the blindfolds were removed. I blinked and looked around. It was a dark, overcast night. The full moon could barely be seen behind the clouds obscuring it. All the other freshmen were there. Bailey had a hilarious case of bed-head. Tony had a Teenage Mutant Ninja Turtles tee shirt on. The sweats that Chad slept in had more holes than fabric to them. It was definitely not our best look.

Kanoa came forward, beaming that happy smile of his. He had a pair of dark jeans and a dark hoody on. I was very jealous of that hoody, for more than one reason.

"Evening, gents," he said. "Every year, the new fish on the team go through this initiation. It's a rite of passage, a tradition—"

"Dude, it's fucking freezing, get on with it," one of the varsity players grumbled.

Kanoa's friends laughed. We initiates nervously joined in. Kanoa flipped the speaker off. "Don't be such a baby, Brian," he said with a grin. He turned back to us. "Fine. Basically, this is where you earn your place on the team for real. Welcome to the seventeenth annual Skinny Dip Guppy Race."

"The what now?" Jimmy asked in the most indignant squeak I'd ever heard.

The varsity players rumbled with laughter. "Out there past the waves, Jacob and Minh are waiting in a boat with a necklace for each of you." He pulled out a radio and said into it, "You're on." A small light blinked on in the dark waves beyond. "The first one to get their necklace and get back wins bragging rights and a week's training with the varsity team."

"Are you insane?" Jimmy croaked. He, like me, was only wearing a pair of soft cotton shorts. "We'll freeze to death."

"No, but it will feel like it," Brian told us. He looked really smug about it.

Kanoa spread his hands. "What are you guys waiting for? The next beach patrol is in ten minutes."

My fellow freshmen looked at each other with varying degrees of horror. No one wanted to go into that water. I sure as fuck didn't. I liked my balls and I didn't want them frozen off.

But then I looked at Kanoa and I saw his quiet encouragement. It was a look I'd seen on his face every time I'd told him I couldn't do another lap or another rep. That stupid thing called pride reared up and told me that it didn't care about the danger to my nuts. I was going to get that necklace and be the first one back, and not because of bragging rights or varsity training. I was going to do it for Kanoa.

Heads turned to me as I shucked my shorts and underwear. I didn't care that my business was hanging out there for anyone to see—I really didn't, which was a big surprise. I turned and raced for the water, exhilarated. I only barely took in the fact that the other guys were following my lead. I wasn't worried about them. This wasn't practice anymore. This was a race and they were about to see what I could do.

The brutally cold water sent a shock through my system. Instead of paralyzing me, though, it energized me. I set my eyes on that light in the darkness and I surged through the water, almost laughing because I felt so insanely free in that moment. This was what I was born to do.

I reached the boat so fast, it startled me. It had seemed much further away. A pair of grinning faces peered out of the darkness. "How's the water?" Minh asked.

"Refreshing," I chattered.

"Here ya go," Jacob said, slipping a leather necklace over my head. Then he rubbed my wet hair like he was petting a dog. Somehow, it didn't offend me. Maybe because the next words out of his mouth were, "You'd better hurry if you want to beat Kanoa's record."

I grinned and shot off back in the direction of the beach even as Bailey reached the boat. He was faster than I had realized. I couldn't slack off. It didn't seem possible that I'd beat Kanoa's time, but you can bet I wanted to try.

Bailey would just….

As I swam along, I thought of Bailey. He worked harder than anyone on the team. He was the first of the guys to approach the weird outsider with an overture of friendship. He took all the cracks about his size and his birthmark with a smile. And he'd done it all without special attention from a varsity swimmer.

I slowed down as I thought of what it would mean to Bailey if he won. I didn't need the training, but if he got to spend a week with the varsity team, he'd be on cloud nine. Everyone would respect him, and no one knows more than me how important that is.

I didn't need to win, I realized. I'd already gotten so much.

Bailey surged ahead of me. I stayed on his tail, not letting him get too far ahead. I wanted him to believe he'd earned it—and he had, just in a different way. When we reached the beach, I stumbled along behind him and watched as the varsity team greeted him with cheers and towels.

He looked back at me, a question in his eyes. I shrugged, doing my best impression of looking annoyed. What I really felt, though, was happy. I was happy for him and I was happy for me. The team misfits had proven themselves.

Kanoa wrapped me in big fluffy towels and handed me a paper cup filled with steaming hot chocolate. To my surprise, he didn't move off to tend to the other swimmers returning to the shore. He left that task to Brian, who was making sure every single swimmer got back.

"You cost me ten bucks," Kanoa complained, sitting next to me.

"Huh?"

"I bet Brian you'd be first in."

"Sorry."

"Yeah, you don't look very sorry," Kanoa said, smiling crookedly.

"I, um, got a cramp."

"Uh huh." He winked at me. "Looking out for your teammates is the sign of a real champion."

That made me squirm. "I was just, you know…."

"You had a cramp." Kanoa looked so proud of me that it was like I had won after all. That brought way more warmth to my insides than the cocoa. "I get it. But just so you know, if you do that because you feel bad for someone on some *other* team, I'll kick your ass."

"Yes, sir." I couldn't stop smiling. It was weird. I'd never been so happy. "I owe you a lot, for helping me."

Kanoa gave me a perplexed look. "You don't owe me anything. All I did was let you train with me."

I laughed. "Dude, you act like that's no big deal. You have no idea…."

"I kind of do," he said, his eyes fixed on the ocean. "Like I said, I was skinny and awkward too, once."

"I can't picture that."

"I burned all the pictures." I laughed. "No, seriously. That was not a good time for me. You're a lot different than I was. I had no confidence at all."

"Like I do?"

"Shit yes. You just do what you want, you don't care what people think. You hang with that Liam guy. I would have been terrified of what people would have thought of me, but you didn't let that stop you. You never once said you couldn't do it, when we were training." He gave me a wry grin. "You complained, sure, who wouldn't? But you never even considered giving up. I had to be pushed by my older brother to get into shape."

I looked down. I'd never really thought being stubborn was a form of courage. "Well, I wanted to make you proud of me."

Why did you say that? I demanded of myself. *Don't make this weird!*

Kanoa was blushing. I could see it even in the limited moonlight. "I don't know why."

I shrugged. I had to change the subject before I made things worse. "It's cold."

Kanoa nodded. "Brian?" he called. "Is everyone back yet?"

"Last one's coming in now."

Kanoa gave me a strange look, like he was considering asking me something. And then he shrugged. "Okay, let's bail."

I was relieved that he let me off the hook so easily. At the same time, though, I really wanted to know what that weird look from him was all about.

CHAPTER 16

Liam was, I think, the only thing that kept me from having a total meltdown. Just when I was about to announce plans to change my name and move to a remote province of China, Liam would crack a joke and I would feel better.

"You're going to kill in that race," Liam assured me as he flipped through one of my comic books.

It was the Friday before D-Day, so my stomach was in knots. I had three days until I had to meet my fate.

I frowned at him. "I'll settle for 'not totally sucking.'"

The secret to happiness in life was, I felt, keeping your expectations reasonable.

"Kanoa probably wouldn't mind if you sucked," Liam remarked with a little smirk.

"Are you kidding? He would kill—" I got the joke a few seconds late. I managed to glare and blush all at the same time. "Will you stop shipping us? It's not going to happen."

"I'm just saying, a hot senior spending all this time with a jittery freshman, there has to be a reason."

"Yeah, it's called the coach asking him to."

"Maybe...."

"Can you just let me crush in peace? Please?"

Liam laughed but made no promises. But of course he wouldn't, because he was Liam. He went back to his comic book for a few minutes and then cast it aside.

"Man, I can't believe we're stuck at home instead of at the Homecoming Dance,"

"Trust me, this is better," I told him. "At least for me. My dance moves are outlawed in twelve states."

Liam cracked a smile. "I got to see that."

I frowned at him. "No."

Liam's eyes lit up with mischief. "Uh uh, you can't keep claiming to be bad at everything without proof. You have to show me."

"I really don't."

He went over to my laptop and called up the music player. "Hmm, let's see, what do we have for playlists? 'Life sux?' 'Love sux?' I'm sensing a theme here."

"At least I'm consistent."

"True. Hey, 'OMG the 80's' I think we have a winner."

"I'm not dancing," I told him.

I thought my tone was pretty firm. That didn't prevent him from yanking me to my feet, though, with a strength I didn't think he had. As the familiar beat of one of my favorite classics warbled out of my laptop's crappy speakers, I folded my arms and backed away from the crazy guy with the infectious smile.

"Come on, feel the beat," Liam coaxed.

I just couldn't hang onto my glower, not with him gyrating and flailing like a fish out of water. It didn't seem possible, but somehow he was actually as bad or worse than me.

"Oh girls just want to have fun," he sang—badly— and danced (if one could call it that) over to me.

"You really don't get the whole 'no' concept, do you?"

"Not when I'm right. Now dance, beyatch."

I did my best to suppress a grin that I felt coming over me. Very, very cautiously, I started to bob my shoulders and sway my arms. Maybe there was a chance I could give him a little token effort and he would leave me alone. Maybe he would tire of the game after a minute or two.

I know, what was I thinking?

Liam started hopping up and down and throwing his hands in the air. I was grateful my mom was at work, considering the noise he was making. I didn't need her coming in and seeing me dancing with *that boy*.

My legs moved as if they had developed a mind of their own. The delight in Liam's face just washed over me like sunshine, making me warm all over. The darkness of my self-doubt just couldn't withstand all that light.

"That's better," Liam approved, swiveling his hips like he had a Hula Hoop around them.

I shook my head even as a laugh bubbled out of me. He was simply irresistible. But even as my seriously lame moves busted loose, he didn't mock me or burst out laughing. He just grinned happily and danced around like the lunatic he was.

The beautiful, weird lunatic that he was....

I thought he'd let me go after the first song, but when Soft Cell's *Tainted Love* came on he crowed, "I love this song!" and danced even more crazily.

I matched him, move for move. We danced as only white boys can—with absolutely no rhythm and no style. But it was fun, at least until the song ended.

And then it got weird.

"Oh Justin, you really are a gay boy," Liam commented around a grin. "*Hold Onto The Night*? Really?"

"Shut up," I told him and turned to tell the computer to skip past Richard Marx, even though it was too late to save my reputation.

"No, come on!" he objected, pulling me back. "Slow dance!"

"Liam...."

"When are you going to learn I always get my way?"

I huffed at him, but his responding look was implacable. He was right. There was never any point in trying to defy him. He was a force of nature. He always won in the end.

He looped his arms around my neck and gave me this evil wink as he swayed back and forth. It felt entirely natural, dancing with him. I put my hands on his hips and swayed with him, just looking down at his face and thinking how amazing he was.

"You're not that bad a dancer," he told me.

"You're not much of an expert."

"Oh no, you did *not* just diss my moves."

I smiled. I had the strangest urge to bring him in close and hold him, which was absolutely not going to happen. I felt my crush starting to break loose from its cage, and I did not want him to see that. That would just be too stupid.

But it was so nice, swaying with him, dancing so close. It was almost like we had gone to the dance together, almost like we were more than friends.

Liam looked up at me with a coy smile on his face. I didn't know what that look meant, but I knew what I wanted it to mean. I knew how things in my head were spiraling out of control and how much that scared the shit out of me. I could almost feel my muscles tensing as I started to lean down towards him.

"Oh, Justin," he vamped and nuzzled into my chest. "You big strong man."

That broke the spell. I pushed him away and turned off the music. I felt Liam staring at me, but I didn't feel like facing him. I didn't want to see him smirking, to know how funny he thought his joke was. And I didn't want to try and explain why I was suddenly out of sorts.

"I was just playing," Liam said.

"I know."

"Dude, what happened? Why is it weird all of a sudden?"

I shook my head. "Never mind."

Liam was quiet for a moment—a very long moment. Liam is never quiet for long, so I guessed he was thinking things over. He was adding up the pieces and trying to figure out why I was being a freak. I hoped that he would decide to drop it and make a joke of things, but that wasn't the sort of night that I was having.

"Oh," he said finally.

"Liam...."

"Dude, it's cool. I'm sorry, I was an ass."

I half-turned, afraid of what I might see on his face. I didn't want things to be weird. I didn't want to have screwed things up again. I didn't want to lose him.

Liam had this adorably perplexed look on his face. "Justin, it's cool. For serious. I just didn't think."

I shrugged a little, allowing a slight glimmer of optimism into my world. "It's not a big deal."

"No, I know, but I still feel bad for making you uncomfortable."

I retrieved my smile from the dark hole it was hiding in. "When has that ever stopped you?"

Liam's lips quirked. "So, we're cool?"

"Well, I am, but you need work."

"Ha! I knew being a jock would go to your head."

He was granting me the only thing I asked for—a free pass out of the conversation. It didn't matter that I had a crush on him. It wasn't going to go anywhere. Talking about it sure wasn't going to make anything better. So it was for the best to just drop it and never, ever bring it up again—*ever*.

CHAPTER 17

I don't think it comes as a surprise to hear that by Monday, I was a nervous wreck. My pessimistic nature imagined about thirty disaster scenarios that ended with the team demanding I commit ritual suicide.

Making matters worse, my mom was there, and Liam and Kanoa. I was grateful for their support, of course, but I didn't feel I needed anyone witnessing the catastrophe that was going to befall me. Knowing they were there only made the lead in my stomach even heavier.

So I was not doing at all well when the meet started. I found myself fantasizing that the school would catch fire or Martians would invade or something— *anything*—to get me out of the competition.

Then the strangest thing happened. Kanoa pulled me aside and just his smile was enough to make my knees stop quaking.

"You feel like you're going to puke?"

I nodded. "If I'd eaten anything today, I would."

Kanoa grinned at me. "I felt the same way my first meet."

I gaped at him. "Really?"

"Seriously."

I didn't feel better, exactly, but some of the mind-numbing terror receded. "What did you do?"

"All that adrenaline you got pumping through you right now? Use it. Go out there and show them what you got."

I stared at him, baffled by how he could be so confident in me. I also couldn't quite figure out why he cared. It wasn't like my performance mattered to his life in any way.

"You got this," he told me and slipped his arm around my bare shoulders and *that* sent fireworks off in my brain, let me tell you.

"Okay," I said, gnawing on my thumbnail. "Okay, I can do this."

As weird as it was that Kanoa was there to buck me up, that wasn't even the strange thing that happened. The really bizarre thing was that when I got up on my springboard, all of the stress and all of the anxiety just went away. I was in a familiar place, since the meet was held at my school. I was doing something I had done dozens of times already. My mind went into hyper focus and I blocked out the crowds and Coach Lancaster and my own team.

I was, as they say, in the zone.

Fearless

I didn't jump before the gun, as so many of my nightmares had predicted I would. My suit did not disintegrate like tissue paper. And Ms. Warner didn't yank me out of the pool to go to a final I hadn't studied for.

I shot into the water like I'd been fired out of a cannon. My limbs fell into the rhythm they had grown so used to. Though I'd only been working out for a little over a month, my muscles had hardened enough that I was able to knife through the water like I was a dolphin or something.

Kanoa had taught me that I wasn't competing against the other swimmers—that I was competing against myself. That was an important lesson, because there was no way I could keep track of the other guys in the water. I would lose precious time trying to figure out if they were ahead or behind me.

But there was one guy in the lane next to me that I was neck and neck with and so I figured it wouldn't hurt to at least try to leave him in my wake. He was fast, though, and every time I took the lead, I only held it for a second or so before he took it back.

I was *not* going to let Kanoa down, though. I was going to give this everything I had, even if that wasn't enough. This wasn't like the beach. Here, I had no reason to hold back. Here, I was going to make Kanoa proud.

My muscles burned as I pushed myself to my very limits and beyond. My useless, clumsy feet chopped into the water in a relentless staccato rhythm. The smell of the chlorinated water filled my nostrils, and its familiarity invigorated me.

When I touched the edge of the pool for the last time, I quickly ripped my goggles off so I could see how I'd done.

Please don't make me have sucked too bad, I begged the Flying Spaghetti monster.

I stared in disbelief, not quite comprehending what I was seeing on the board. It just didn't make any sense to me. I was sure it had to be a mistake.

But the roaring of the crowd behind me only confirmed the impossible.

I came in first.

No, seriously, I came in *first*.

I climbed out of the pool and instantly I was surrounded by my teammates, who patted me on the back and called me "the man" and crowed and generally acted like I was a hero.

And that was all great and everything. It really was. But it was when I looked up at the stands and I saw Liam grinning at me and giving me a thumbs-up of approval that I really felt like screaming in triumph.

The team overall did pretty good. Jimmy, Chad and Bailey all took first place too. So the team's mood was really good. I mean, it wasn't like we were suddenly school royalty or anything. We were still the Frosh-Soph swim team, so it wasn't like people showered us with presents wherever we went, but we got a few fist bumps and high-fives in the halls.

With things going so well, the dread I used to experience every time I awoke for school disappeared. It was a new and very comfortable feeling and I basked in it. I was tripping a lot less and I'd gotten much better at catching myself, so I was much less of a localized disaster waiting to happen. Being on friendly terms with my teammates meant I could give them those silent nods we guys like to exchange that mean stuff I can't explain without being cited for violating the guy code. Those little nods made other people see me as something other than the weird kid, and that made school much easier to deal with.

Training with Kanoa continued, which surprised me. I figured he would tell me he needed to focus on his own training or something. I wouldn't have held it against him. He'd done so much for me and it wasn't like I could cling to him forever.

But he didn't ditch me and I sure wasn't going to ask to be sent away. I mean, seeing him in a Speedo several times a week was kind of like live-action porn. Okay, no, I'll be honest. As hot as *that* was, the best part was just hanging out with him.

The only thing that soured it was the way his girlfriend kept showing up and intruding on my Kanoa time. I'm an only child. I don't really do well with sharing. Couldn't she restrict her drama to when she had him the other twenty-three hours a day?

When I saw them together, they always seemed to be arguing. And that annoyed me. Kanoa was about the most laid-back, chill dude I have ever met. So I couldn't imagine what she did that got him so upset, but I was sure he didn't deserve it.

Finally, I got annoyed enough that I said something. We'd been hanging out for weeks now, so I thought maybe it would be okay. Someone sure had to tell him he could do better.

"So, your girlfriend seemed upset," I said as we stretched before our run. The girl in question had just left after another argument.

"Huh?" he asked.

"Sorry, I didn't overhear. I just saw you two arguing."

Kanoa frowned. "Justin...."

I forced a shrug as my confidence crumbled. Maybe I really *didn't* have the right to say anything. I didn't want to piss him off. And I really didn't want him thinking it was because I was jealous of her, even though I was, but he wasn't allowed to know that.

"It's none of my business."

"Dude, Aolani's my sister."

I stared at him and felt a stupid rush of relief. So what if *this* hot girl wasn't his girlfriend? What difference did that really make? That just meant there was some *other* hot girl somewhere I had not yet met.

"Oh," was all I said.

"Her boyfriend just dumped her. She's always doing this. She picks out the absolute worst guy and then is all shocked when he turns out to be a loser. I swear, we may be twins but I sometimes have no idea what goes on in that head of hers."

"Twins?"

"Yep."

It took me a little bit to remember that Aolani was the girl Liam was interested in. So the fact that she was single *and* related to Kanoa meant I had two reasons to celebrate. That brightened up my whole morning.

"I have good news," I told Liam in English.

"Yeah?"

I explained to him about Aolani and that she had just been dumped. "You could swoop in, you know? Be her knight in shining armor, like."

Liam bit his lower lip. "Maybe."

"What do you mean, 'maybe'?"

"Dude, you don't ask a girl out right after she's been dumped. Then you're just the rebound guy."

"But—"

"Just drop it, Justin," he grumbled.

It sounded like a lame rationalization to me. Of course, I had to admit I knew nothing about dating and even less about girls. Liam could be right. I didn't even know there *was* such a thing as rebound.

So I left it alone, figuring I would just bug him about it later. It wasn't like I could *force* him to ask her out.

Even with my life improving, I didn't fail to notice that Liam's mood continued to darken. I noticed because I wanted to share the good turn things were taking with him. He'd suffered along with all my stupid drama. I wanted him to share in the good times too. But he started blowing me off for our afternoon hang-outs and missing more classes.

He wouldn't tell me why, which worried and confused me. I didn't think we had any secrets left between us. I gave him his space, but I didn't like being helpless. He had given me so much, I wanted to do something for him to show how grateful I was.

Inspiration hit one day when I spotted Aolani at the drinking fountain. Liam was still making excuses for not asking Aolani out, so I made a really bold decision. I would do it for him.

"Um, Aolani?"

She paused in her drinking and gave me the sort of smile that I knew would devastate any straight guy. "Hey, you're my brother's friend, right? Justin?"

My brain got sidetracked by the idea that Kanoa talked about me to his sister. I hadn't dared hope that he thought of me outside of practice. What did that mean? And what all did he say? And we were friends? That was huge!

"What's up?" Aolani prodded.

I glanced beyond her to her two friends. Girls and their packs, I just didn't understand it. Jen was texting madly, her face so intent I had to assume she was telling someone how to disarm a bomb attached to a school bus full of kids. Keisha was checking her make-up, which seemed flawless to me.

"Um, can I talk to you a sec?"

"Sure."

There was a smug confidence to her look, like she knew what was coming. I stepped away from her gang, leading her a few feet away so we could chat without her friends giving me the stink eye—or worse, *giggling.* In my experience, a girl can pack a lot of meanness into a giggle.

I hoped she didn't think I was going to ask her out. I mean, if I was going to ask a girl out, it would probably be someone like Aolani. She was nice to look at, with the same bronze skin her brother had and pretty, gentle eyes. She also had curves—that is to say, she wasn't fat, but she had meat on her bones, giving her hips and cleavage a little more definition. Personally, that waif look freaks me all the fuck out.

I can appreciate girls without wanting to do them, you know.

"Do you know my friend Liam?"

She looked confused. "The stoner?"

I sighed. Liam really needed to work on his rep. "He's not…. He only does a little weed now and then."

Aolani laughed. It was a pretty sound—honest and unrestrained. "Justin, I'm not a narc. I party too, with the right crowd."

I lowered my hackles. "Liam's a really good guy. He's like, the best guy, really, though you wouldn't know it to look at him."

"Is he your boyfriend?"

"What? Why would you even say that?" I asked, terrified to even speculate why she might think that.

That smirk of hers was back. "No reason."

I was completely off balance. I didn't even want to go out with her myself and she'd turned me into a floundering idiot. How did straight guys ever manage it?

"Uh, anyway, he really wants to go out with you."

Aolani studied me for a second. "For real? You're asking me out *for* him?"

"Well, I was just seeing if you would be interested...."

Her eyes sparkled with mystery. "For serious?"

"Uh, is that bad?"

"No, it's cute."

Cute sounded bad, but I decided to not argue with her. At least she wasn't being mean about it. I could see why Liam liked her. She wasn't dumb or vain. She didn't pretend to be anything but what she was.

"So...?"

"I'll go out with him, if he asks me," Aolani said.

I relaxed a little. "Okay," I said, smiling anyway. "Thanks."

"There isn't anything else you wanted to ask me?" That mystery in her eyes deepened.

I gave her a blank stare. "Huh?"

She gave me another merry laugh. "Okay, I guess not. Nice to meet you, Justin."

I watched her rejoin her friends, completely confused. I really did feel bad for straight guys in that moment. Girls weren't just another gender, they were an alien race, with customs and language all their own.

I was glad that this was the closest I would ever come to having to ask one out.

Even though the whole encounter had left me confused and unsettled, I was at least happy that I had secured a date for Liam with his dream girl. At least one of us had a shot with their ideal date. I had no doubt Liam would charm Aolani easily with his Liam-ness.

"Hey, dude," I said as I sat next to Liam in History.

The class was still settling in around us, so we had a minute. Liam looked tired and grouchy, but he forced a smile for me. "Hey."

"So, uh, did you know that Aolani is Kanoa's sister?"

He shook his head. "No. You want to double date?"

Holy fuck yes. "Very funny. I talked to her about you. She's interested."

"Interested in what?"

"You, stupid."

His weary smile vanished. "Why did you do that?"

"I was being your wingman."

It had been a while since I'd seen Liam's temper, but it was all over him now. "I don't need a wingman. If I want to ask someone out, I will."

"Then why haven't you?"

"I have other shit on my mind."

"Why are you being such a psycho?" I asked. "You did this for me, remember?"

"That was different."

"How?"

Liam glowered at me. "Because you're so scared you won't even think of asking some dude out."

I flinched. "That's not true. Dude, what has gotten into you?"

"You just shouldn't have done this," he told me. "It's not a good time."

I really couldn't believe the way he was acting. I was handing him his dream girl with a pink bow on her head. "You're so full of shit. You talk a big game, but when it comes down to it, you're just as scared as me. For all your talk, you're just too scared she'll say no."

"Fuck you, Justin. I don't need this shit."

And with that, he grabbed his stuff and left. I stared after him, shocked and angry and sad and worried and so many things I couldn't even list them. My best friend had just stormed out, and I didn't know if he was ever coming back—to school or to me.

CHAPTER 18

By the time I got home, I was in a really foul mood. I was angry with Liam for overreacting to my attempt to be a good friend. I was even more pissed at myself for screwing up another friendship—the best one of my life so far.

Why couldn't I ever stop fucking things up?

There was no one I could ask that question. Liam was who I would go to, but what did you do when your best friend *was* the problem? I sure as hell couldn't talk to my mom—the smug satisfaction on her face would only make things a million times worse.

I paced the length of my room, kicking clothes out of my way. There was one person, I realized, staring at my computer. I hadn't actually talked to Hawaii in a week, I'd been so busy. I didn't know if he even came on anymore. But it was worth a try. I had to talk to someone or I would lose my mind.

Luckily, he was on. I pinged him instantly, not playing any games.

> JustM3*87: Hey dude.
> Hawaii5*9: Dude, where you been?
> JustM3*87: Busy, sry.
> Hawaii5*9: No prob, was just worried. Everything okay?
> JustM3*87: Not rly, could use a friend. Want to meet up?

I knew it was stupid—even suicidal, but I didn't care. Playing it safe only ever got me hurt anyway, so what difference did it make?

> Hawaii5*9: For real?
> JustM3*87: Yeah.

As much as I wanted to believe that Hawaii was the chill teen dude he was online, the rational part of me knew that Hawaii was a fifty-year-old guy with back-hair and a beer belly, but I threw that part of me into the basement of my mind and locked the door. It was time to do something crazy.

We'd never discussed meeting, though I knew we lived in the same county. We'd never talked specifics. I think neither of us wanted to come off as a Stalker. We both knew that for teens, meeting guys online was a good way to wind up in the trunk of a car.

> JustM3*87: You there?

Hawaii5*9: Yep. Know where the Starbucks is on 9th and Juniper?
JustM3*87: No, but I have Google.

I checked the location and bus routes.

JustM3*87: Meet you there at 5?
Hawaii5*9: Ok. How will I know you?
JustM3*87: I'll be reading Dreamscape.
Hawaii5*9: :) Ok.

You're a crazy moron and you're going to die, I told myself. That didn't stop me from changing my shirt and zipping out the door. I can't explain what I was thinking. My head was a total mess. I couldn't fix the Liam situation and that drove me nuts.

I don't have a coffee habit—like I could afford one. I got the smallest, cheapest thing they had and settled at a table by the window. I had no idea what Hawaii looked like so I just watched every customer who walked in the door. College dudes with their girlfriends, business guys with briefcases, a pair of mechanics on their break, they all came and went. The first guy that came in by himself made me want to duck into the bathroom.

You can call me all the terrible names you want, but I don't want to date a guy who's older than my grandpa. Not my thing.

The old guy flirted with the girl behind the counter and then got his beverage and left. I breathed a sigh of relief.

Anxiety gave way to boredom, and even that eventually faded before the onslaught of disappointment. Five o'clock became six, and by seven it was clear that

Hawaii wasn't coming. I felt like a total loser. I wouldn't have even said, categorically, that being stood up was better than winding up in the trunk of a car.

When I got home, I found Hawaii's profile had been deleted. Apparently, meeting me had been such a horrifying idea that I'd scared him right off the Internet.

Life can really suck sometimes, you know?

Liam wasn't at school the next day, which actually didn't surprise me. What did surprise me was how lonely everything seemed without him. I knew I could probably find Bailey or one of the other guys on the team and figure out some way to hang with them, but I didn't want to. The truth was, I knew that even being surrounded by the guys, I would still feel lonely because they weren't Liam. I'd have to be on my guard around them, have to watch what I said and how I acted. It would be awful.

I spent the day figuring out a good groveling strategy. Pride is a useless thing, really. All it does is make you too stupid to do the things you need to do to fix what's broken. My friendship with Liam was broken. I didn't know how or why, but I was going to make it clear to him I'd do whatever he wanted to make things right.

So when I saw I'd missed his call while I was at practice, I rushed to call him back. Anna answered, and she sounded even more tired than usual.

"It was actually me that called, I hope that's okay."

I went from confusion to worry in a microsecond. "Is Liam okay?"

"He had a rough chemo this morning. He's feeling pretty sick. I'm keeping him home for a few days. Would you mind bringing his schoolwork over? I called and the admin office said they'd have it waiting to be picked up."

"Of course."

Me, being an idiot, hadn't thought to tie his recent moodiness to chemo. He always made it out like the treatments were no big deal, just a minor nuisance. Had things been worse lately and he hadn't told me? If so, why not? I would have understood.

Or did he think I wouldn't? That possibility crushed me.

I picked up his books and assignments and took the bus to his apartment building because it was too much to carry on my bike. I also called my mom to let her know I would be home late. She was keeping even closer tabs on me than before. I think she was worried that I was going to run off and join a Pride Parade.

Anna welcomed me in and she really did look like she hadn't slept in a couple of days. "I really appreciate this, Justin. We've only the one car and Mike—"

"It's no problem," I told her. I put the pile of books and papers on the counter. "After all you've done for me, this is nothing."

"How are things with your mom, sweetie?"

The way she said "sweetie" had a weird effect on me, like I wanted to hug her or something. It had been a while since my mom and I had been on hugging terms. We were still working on not-screaming-at-each-other terms.

"We're working through it," I replied. That was about the only way to describe it.

"Well, you're always welcome here."

"Thanks." I looked in the direction of Liam's room. "Can I see him?"

"I think he's sleeping."

Fearless

"Just for a second?" I pleaded.

Anna nodded, passing a hand over her eyes. "The doctors say the more intense chemo is helping, just not as fast as we were hoping for. He's trying to be brave about it—you know Liam."

"Yeah…."

"Yeah...." Anna's smile was so terribly sad. I had never seen so much pride and so much sorrow in one expression before. "He never wants me to know how bad he's feeling." She sniffled. "But I think he's having a hard time with it."

"Um, why don't I sit with him for a while? You look like you could use a nap."

Anna laughed, but there was a shaky, warbling note to it. "He has to take his meds in a little bit."

"Tell me what and when and I'll take care of it."

A single tear escaped the corner of her eye. "You're a saint."

"I don't think they make gay saints."

That made her laugh. "Okay, let me show you what he needs to take…."

Once I had the information, I shooed her off to bed. Then I crept into Liam's room, being as careful as I could to make no noise. I knew from experience that sleep was the best refuge when you felt miserable, so I didn't want to wake him.

The shades were drawn, so the room was completely dark. I saw Sully's head pop up, a shadow amongst shadows. But he recognized me and quickly went back to sleep at Liam's feet.

Once my eyes had adjusted, I looked at my best friend's sleeping form and was struck by how small he seemed. I knew he was shorter than me, of course, but that fact had kind of disappeared behind the bombastic persona of Liam. He was so full of energy, so full of life, that he seemed like a giant to me—a god towering over us mere mortals.

Curled up and asleep, he looked unnervingly small and frail. He barely took up a fourth of his queen-sized bed. He was so thin—scary thin. I had never noticed before because I'd been almost that skinny. Now, thanks to swimming and eating better, I was filling out. Liam, by contrast, seemed to be getting more frail.

I realized this was Liam without his armor. This was the Liam he didn't want anyone to see. Was that why he had pushed me away? Because he hadn't wanted me to see this?

I sat in the chair next to his bed and just watched him sleep. Even though he was out of it, being there with him made that lonely feeling go away. It was ridiculous and I knew it, but having him nearby put my world back on its axis.

When the clock hit the time Anna had given me, I reached out and took one of Liam's hands in mine. He stirred, eyes fluttering open. I watched as he took stock of his situation; that I had defied my exile, that I was seeing him at his most vulnerable, that I knew now why he had been such a dick to me. So many emotions swirled in his green eyes. I could almost, but not quite, pick them all out.

When he spoke, all he said was, "Hey."

I smiled, because he was the master of downplaying things. "Hi. Time for your meds."

"Mmkay," he murmured.

I got him his Gatorade and the proper pills, being very careful to be sure I got the right ones. I knew Anna was trusting me an awful lot and I didn't want to screw it up. I also didn't even want to think what would happen if I messed up his meds.

Liam sat up to take his pills, drinking down half of the Gatorade. Then he collapsed, like that exertion had been too much for him. His weakness, frankly, scared me. I wasn't used to seeing him beaten down like this.

He surprised me by taking my hand again. The look on his face was kind of shy, and yet kind of coy too.

"Are you giving me my sponge bath later?"

"I'd be happy to," I told him, waggling my eyebrows.

"Pervert."

"And then some."

Liam giggled and coughed. I found a straw so he wouldn't have to sit up again and gave him more Gatorade. He nursed on that for a little bit, looking embarrassed. I took it back when he handed it to me, being sure to cap it so it didn't spill. I didn't know what to say. I was completely freaked out and trying my best to not show it.

"I told you I turn into a whiny bitch after chemo."

"Oh please." I rolled my eyes.

He bit his lower lip. "You wanna come up here with me?"

"Okay."

I moved to sit on the edge of the bed, but he pulled me in and wrapped around me like some kind of bony python. I didn't know what to do, so I just held him, running my hands up and down his bare back. It's what my mom did when I was a kid and feeling sick.

"Thanks for coming," he murmured in a soft voice. "Means a lot."

"That's what friends are for."

"I'm sorry about before." He sounded so lost. "I didn't mean to be a dick. I've just been freaking, a little."

I shrugged—as best as I could, anyway, with Liam wrapped around me. "Forget it."

Liam sniffled. "Lou is really kicking my ass this time."

The simple mention of that name sent a chill up my spine. "Your mom says you're getting better."

"Doesn't feel like it." He shook against me. "I'm lucky I met you."

"Nah, I'm the lucky one."

"Shut up, I'm complimenting you."

"Sorry."

"That's better." He trembled a little more. "I only wanted one friend, you know. Just one, not a whole pack. One guy to hang with. And I found this awesome dude…."

"I'm not awe—"

"Shut *up*," he ordered, his voice a crackly warble. "I'm trying to explain shit."

"Sorry."

"It's kind of…. Well, it was selfish. Because I figured Lou was going to get me this time, and whatever friend I made would be sad. So, I'm sorry."

Panic clawed at my heart. "You're getting better."

He laughed. It turned into a sob. And then he was crying so hard his whole body was convulsing against me. I held onto him, totally ripped apart by how much pain he was in. There was nothing I could do—not one God damn fucking thing.

If life could break someone as brave as Liam, what chance did a pathetic loser like me have?

His wrenching, wracking sobs went on and on like he might never stop. I hugged him tight to me and tried to soothe him, but I felt so helpless. I didn't know what to say. Everything I thought of just sounded idiotic in my head.

Little by little, the convulsions eased. His tears stuttered to a halt. And then he just shivered against me, his breath hitching.

"Fucking Lou," Liam choked out, wiping his eyes. "He turns me into such a crybaby."

I looked into those moist green eyes, and my heart ached. "You don't have to be strong all the time."

That made him tear up again. He curled up against me and sniffled. "I just get so tired sometimes. It never seems to end and sometimes…. Sometimes I just want it to."

Sometimes I just want it to….

"I can't even imagine."

"Yeah…." Liam let out a shaky breath. "It was sweet, what you did with Aolani. It was never that I was scared she would say no. It's just…. I don't want too many people to miss me when I'm gone. I don't want to do that to them."

"Oh, Liam…." I blinked away hot tears. The defeat in his voice was like a knife in my stomach. "You're not going anywhere. You're too tough."

"Not that you'd know it to look at me right now."

"Shut up, it's my turn now."

A dusty, dry laugh escaped him. "Okay, Tina."

"Don't call me that," I grumbled.

"Sorry."

He didn't sound sorry.

I took a deep breath and struggled to find the words to explain, to make him understand what was in my heart. It wasn't easy, because there were so many emotions twisting me up inside. But in their midst was a core idea and I wanted to get it across to him.

"You owe it to people to let them know you. Because knowing you has changed my life."

Liam wiped his runny nose. "Yeah?"

"Yeah."

I took off my shirt to give him something to wipe his face. It was already a loss from his storm of weeping anyway. When he settled back down, pillowing his head on my chest, it felt really nice—intimate in a way that was somehow not sexual. I was too much of a mess to figure out how that worked.

"You can't live your life waiting for Lou to get you," I told him, working really hard to keep my voice even. The idea of Liam dying was something I couldn't handle at all. "If you put everything on hold … friends, girls, whatever, then you're dead already, aren't you?"

"Who died and made you Dr. Phil?" he asked, smiling up at me.

"Plagiarist."

Liam settled back down. "You may be right. I thought I was the brains in this friendship."

"That was a dumb thing to think."

Liam laughed, if only briefly. "Can you do me a favor?"

"Sure."

"Can you smuggle me in a cheeseburger and fries?" His moist eyes radiated hope.

I laughed. "No. Your mom would kill me."

"Come on. I'll show you my dick…."

"Seen it."

"Damn." Liam snuggled into me. "Can you stay over?"

"I'm not going anywhere," I told him.

I wasn't, either. I was getting into the trenches with him. Lou was going to have to fight both of us. And we were going to kick his ass.

CHAPTER 19

It was a few days before Liam came back to school. But when he did, he was the Liam I knew and…. Yeah, you've probably guessed, haven't you? I was totally in love with him. Even my heart is stupid. Falling in love with my straight best friend, does it get any more cliché?

So, when he started going out with Aolani, I had all these ugly and really inappropriate jealous feelings. They were stupid and embarrassing, so I just buried them. I did it because Liam was happy, and that was the only thing that mattered. I wouldn't allow myself to ruin things for him.

And hey, I still had my hand, so I could cope.

It was also kind of adorable how excited he was. He just couldn't stop talking about her. And even though it made me crazy with jealousy, I loved hearing how well he and Aolani were getting along. I think that's called masochism.

I also had my hands full with my team. We were doing really well, and when the meets broke for winter break, we looked good for getting into the semi-finals. This had the weird effect of bringing out my dormant competitive nature, which surprised me all to hell.

The team started to regret making me captain once I started pushing them really hard in practice. I wasn't doing anything to them that Kanoa hadn't done to me, but there was still a lot of whining about it.

The holidays came and went. Nothing really special happened. My mom and I were too broke to do much for Christmas, so we just had a nice dinner and watched TV together which was pleasant and (more importantly) normal. It was great to get closer to that status quo my coming out had shattered.

Liam got better, or at least stronger. Having him back to his old self was even better than my unexpected success in the pool. Even though he still liked to embarrass me and sometimes make me do things I didn't want to do. In fact, as February got underway, he hatched a scheme that did both of those things at the same time.

"So, Aolani and I are going to the Valentine's Day dance."

"Well, duh," I said, ignoring that part of me that wanted to throw a tantrum. "You two are a total item."

"That's true!" Liam was almost skipping along as he walked me to the bus that would take me to the next meet. "I am the man."

"You are," I agreed. "A short, skinny man."

He stuck his tongue out at me. "So, now you need a date."

"I think Rosy is shy about crowds."

He laughed. "Do gay guys get to call their hands Rosy?"

"I'll ask the cabal when we meet next."

"So, who are we going to get you to go with? We've only got two weeks until the dance."

I shook my head. "I thought I made it clear I'm not allowed on dance floors."

"Doesn't matter, you're going."

"Oh, you think so?" I gave him a little shove.

"I know so."

I rolled my eyes. "I can't even get Internet trolls to prey on me. I think dating is not in my future."

I'd told him about the disaster with Hawaii. He had insisted on focusing on how great it was that I actually tried to go on something like a date. He was so impossible that way, always looking for the best in a situation.

"I'm not kidding about this, Justin," Liam told me with a look that was so intense it made me worry. "You find a date or I'll find one for you. I *will* start asking everyone here with testicles if I have to."

I wished I could believe he was kidding. "Going to a dance with a guy will out me to the whole school."

"So?"

"So, I want to live to see sixteen."

"Dude, this isn't like the Dark Ages or the nineties or something. A lot of people don't care."

Zach cared. "Why is this so important to you?"

"Because it is. Now stop being a baby. You're an athlete. Demand the virgin sacrifices that you're due."

"You're completely nuts."

"Maybe. But don't think I won't carry through on my threat."

With those ominous words ringing in my ears, he told me to have a good race and that he'd meet me there. I watched him go, my teeth further mangling my thumbnail. I really didn't like the idea of him asking every dude in school if they'd go out with me. But Liam was just ballsy (and insane) enough to do it.

"Dude, why do you hang with that loser?"

I hadn't noticed Bailey come up to me. "Liam?" I glared at him, instantly furious. "He's not a loser." He flinched like he was getting ready for me to punch him. I sighed, realizing how angry I sounded. I was still working on my people skills. "Sorry. It's just.... If you knew him, you'd know he's totally cool."

"Really? He looks like a gang-banger."

I actually managed to laugh, remembering how I'd thought the same thing when meeting Liam. "He does, but he's not."

Bailey fell into step with me, his hands in his pockets. "How'd you meet? I mean, you know, you don't look like.... I mean you two don't seem to fit."

"That's a long story. And it's kind of funny. I'll tell you sometime."

Bailey.... Bailey really was a cute guy. I'd noticed that more and more. I'd also noticed that he never talked about girls. So I'd had my suspicions about him, and even some vague interest in acting on those suspicions. It was just that I liked to reserve those crazy ideas for the world of "someday." That way, I wasn't saying no but I wasn't committing to anything that would wind up humiliating me.

But Liam's threat had forced me to look at the idea more seriously. Bailey *was* cute. Sure, he was short and had braces and he had the same acne we teens are all plagued with, but he was still an attractive guy. Maybe…. *Maybe….*

The very idea of asking him out made my stomach do somersaults. On top of the fact that it would out me, which was terrifying, there was also the really good chance he'd say no, which was worse.

Just ask him. That's what Liam would do.

Liam…. This was all his fault. I shouldn't have to jeopardize the tiny fraction of peace I'd built in my life. Things were fine now. Why did he want to throw a grenade into the apple cart? Why couldn't we just leave things alone?

I had a lot of really good, solid rationalizations for why I should be staying home the night of the dance. What sucked was that I knew none of them would mean shit to Liam. He would go off and start asking random strangers to go with me.

I tried all through the meet to find the words (and the courage) to talk to Bailey. Each time I started to form a sentence though, it bogged down in my throat and refused to come out.

Would Liam accept total vocal paralysis as an excuse? Probably not.

"Bailey, can I talk to you a sec?" someone asked him after we got back from the competition—someone using my voice.

I'd come in third, which had been awful. But it was still better than most of the rest of the team. It really hurt us in the standings and it seriously demoralized us. That made me want to do this even less, but Liam's threat could not be ignored.

"Sure!" He slung his backpack over his shoulder and followed me somewhere I hoped my humiliation would not be witnessed. "What's up?"

Fearless

"Um…." *I hate you, Liam.* "I was wondering…." *Why did you do this to me?* "I mean, I hope it's cool to ask…." *This is such a nightmare.* "Are you g— Um, are you gay? Because I am, and uh, so I was wondering if—" *Kill me now!* "You wanted to go to the dance with me?"

Bailey's eyes widened. "Dude!"

Shit shit shit! I'm going to get you for this, Liam. "Er, forget—"

"Dude, sorry, it's cool. I just…. I was wondering if you were and now I know."

I didn't feel any better. "Is that…? Does that freak you out?"

"Freak me out? Dude, I'm so totally flattered. I'd so go with you, but I'm going with my boyfriend."

I stared at him. Of all the responses I'd been prepared for, that wasn't on my list. "Your...?"

Bailey nodded. "I would so go with you if I were single."

The sting of rejection was muted by my relief that he was at least not pissed at me. "Well, uh, okay then."

It wasn't the worst response to my asking him out, all things considered. And he had said he would have gone out with me if he were single. So, once my heart started beating normally, I actually didn't feel too bad about the situation. In fact, while I'd made a total hash of it, I was kind of proud of myself for taking the chance.

I still needed to pummel Liam for pushing me into this situation, though.

With Bailey no longer a possibility, I had no idea who else to ask. I didn't know too many people at school—there were two thousand students and I was a freshman, after all. Aside from the rumors about Mr.

Richards, the chemistry teacher, I didn't know of any other gay people at school. Mr. Richards wasn't my type, just in case that wasn't obvious.

I told Liam about Bailey, which made him happy but did not get me out from under his threat. It just bought me some time before he became my own personal pimp. I made a brief attempt to argue with him again—brief because it was futile.

I was going to the dance. He wasn't changing his mind.

It wasn't that I didn't *want* a date. If some cute guy asked me out, I'd say yes in a heartbeat. But having to be the one to ask? Having to track down the other gay guys at school? It was a huge task. And it was probably going to get me killed. Zach had proven to me that straight guys don't much like being asked if they're into dudes.

CHAPTER 20

We did our best. We really did. It would have been easier if we had screwed up or slacked off or gotten lazy or something. Every single Frosh-Soft guy did his very best, though, and that made it harder to bear. When you know you gave it everything you had and the other teams were just better, well, it leaves you with an empty feeling.

Lancaster gave us a really nice speech about how proud he was of us. Looking around at Tony and Bailey and Jon and everyone, though, I could tell none of us felt any better. Even Jimmy looked depressed.

I thought maybe as the captain I should say something, but I couldn't think of anything to say that the coach hadn't covered. We did our best and now it was over. We'd made it as far as the semi-finals and that was going to have to be good enough.

"Party at my place!" Brian told us as we boarded the bus.

"What for?" Chad muttered. "We lost."

"Dude, this was the first Frosh-Soft team to get to the Semis in four years. You guys got a lot to celebrate. So the varsity guys are throwing you a party," Brian explained.

"Say you're coming," Kanoa urged me, appearing at my left.

I really didn't feel like it. I just wanted to go home and hide in my room and brood. I could see the rest of the guys felt the same way. And then I realized that the party was just what they needed—we needed—and that was why Kanoa was asking me. He needed me to get the guys on board.

No, I still had no idea why anyone listened to me.

"That sounds great," I said, hoping my fake cheer was believable. "Come on, guys, we've earned it."

Bailey frowned at me for a moment and then changed gears and flashed his braces. "Yeah, we did. We kicked ass. It's not our fault Grant High has a pack of 'roid freaks on their team."

The guys shared a laugh. And that was all it took. Everyone agreed to go and rides and directions were all settled.

Brian lived in the neighborhood I used to live in— the one with cookie-cutter houses and perfect lawns and two cars in every driveway. It made me homesick for a place that was no longer my home. Basically, it was a bad place for me to go with the mood I was in.

But it was really cool of the varsity guys to do it for us. They threw together a barbecue, the pool was heated, and there was great music. They even had these lame tiki torches that made it feel like a luau. A bunch of people from school showed up. I wanted to enjoy it, but it was so hard. Because it felt like the victory celebration my guys deserved but couldn't have.

"Next year," Kanoa said, coming up next to me and pressing a soda into my hand.

He stood next to me as I leaned against a pillar on the back deck, watching the festivities. His warmth, his scent, they were more comforting than I wanted to admit. Kanoa had never once made me feel bad for any of my screw-ups. I'd never even caught the slightest hint of disappointment in his pretty almond eyes.

"Next year, we're taking the trophy," I said with a fierceness that kind of shocked me.

"Damn right," Kanoa agreed. "You did really good, Justin. I know, it sucks. Losing sucks hard. And you feel like crap now. But try and remember how many other guys you left in your wake."

I gave him a smile, because he always seemed to know the right thing to say. "I really wanted to win."

"Well, yeah."

"No, you don't get it." I fiddled with the tab on my soda can. "I've never been competitive. I've never been good enough at anything to bother competing. I never knew what it was like, you know, that feeling of being a winner."

Kanoa didn't laugh, thankfully. He put his hand on my shoulder. "You'll get that trophy."

The mere touch of him made me tingle and sweat. "Yeah, but...." *Oh fuck it.* "I wanted to win it for you."

Kanoa looked adorably confused. "Huh?"

"You made me a winner," I told him. It sounded stupid and corny, but I didn't know how else to say it. "I never would have won anything if you hadn't put in all that time and don't tell me it wasn't anything. It was huge. You took this stupid, scared-shitless freshman and you helped him become something."

"Justin.... You always had it in you."

I laughed. "Maybe, but you made it happen."

He turned to face me full-on, his expression a wealth of conflicting emotions. "It's sweet that you wanted to win for me. I just don't understand why."

"Because I have a huge crush on you."

He stared at me. I stared back at him, horrified by my audacity.

"That came out wrong," I said in the worst attempt at covering ever. *Yeah, and how was that supposed to come out?*

Kanoa was gaping at me. He didn't look horrified, thankfully. He also didn't have that look of disgust Zach had showed at the idea of some guy crushing on me. Kanoa honestly just looked like he had no idea how to respond.

"It's cool if you hate me now," I said, looking down at my feet.

"I couldn't hate you, Justin."

Kanoa continued to stare blankly at me for a long time. I tried to think of a joke or something to move us past the awkwardness I had introduced into the nice conversation we'd been having. Liam would have one. But my mind was blank.

"You remind me so much of me," Kanoa breathed. "But so much braver. You never back down. It was so easy to crush on you." *Say what now?* My heart did a few somersaults. "Then when I saw you in Starbucks and I knew you were the guy I was also crushing on online, I freaked out."

"Wait, what?" I stared at him. "You're Hawaii?"

Kanoa gave me a guilty look. "Yeah."

Fearless

I was now so very confused. Excited, thrilled, overjoyed, but impossibly befuddled. "I waited for you for hours."

Kanoa looked shamefaced. "I'm sorry."

"Just…. Why? I mean, if you liked me…."

"I'm still kind of, well mostly, in the closet. A couple of my friends know, but my family doesn't and they would kill me. I was planning to wait until college…." He looked back out at the party. "When you asked to meet, I almost said no. I figured you were either some creep or you were a guy I'd want to date, and neither of those options were any good. Because I can't date. I can't."

"Then why did you agree to meet?"

"Because I was lonely," he admitted. "Brian is always talking about his girlfriend. And Minh brags about the girls he goes out with. And I just wonder sometimes what it would be like."

My hand shook as it sought out his. He gripped it in response, offering me a melancholy smile. "I know what you mean," I told him. "I get lonely too."

He bit his lower lip. "It was totally crappy of me to ditch you at Starbucks. I just…. I saw the guy I'd gotten to know and like in real life and realized he was also my online boyfriend and it got too real. I panicked."

That sounded so familiar. It was exactly the sort of dumb thing I would do. "Well, don't do that again." He laughed. "I don't suppose you want to go to the V-day dance thing with me," I said, trying to make it sound like it was no big deal either way, even though my entire sense of self-worth was bound up in those words.

Kanoa flinched, his eyes finding mine. "I'd love to go to the dance with you, Justin. Like, you have no idea. But I can't…. If my family finds out…."

~ 185 ~

Something suddenly occurred to me, and it made me grin from ear to ear. "I think your sister already knows."

"She does not." Terror flashed in his eyes. "Why would you think that?"

"When I talked to her, I think she thought I was going to ask about you. She didn't seem freaked at all."

Kanoa chewed on a knuckle. The gesture was too adorable to describe. "That would explain some of the things she's said…."

I reached out to turn his face to me. Liam had taught me how to be strong, how to look into the eyes of the thing that scares you and grin. I felt free from doubt and all my hang-ups and general lameness.

"Kanoa, I know a lot of ignorant jackasses don't like gays. I know my mom wishes I was straight. Your parents may not like you being gay, either. But the question is, do you want to live your life for them? Is that going to make you happy?"

He stared into my eyes like he was mesmerized. "No."

I stroked his cheek with my thumb. He was so beautiful there in the flickering light from the tiki torches, his face now devoid of guile and pretense. "Go to the dance with me?"

He bit his lip and stared into my eyes with a longing that I felt was misplaced but so incredibly flattering. "Okay."

I grinned and somehow didn't make an idiot of myself by letting out an excited whoop. I was learning, you see.

I leaned in. My heart pounded in my chest. His eyes searched my face as he continued to worry at his lip—and his lips were my target. I canted my head to the side and smiled at him. He smiled shyly back and edged forward, like he was scared of getting burned.

"Ew, get a room," Aolani said as she passed us by.

Kanoa started and drew back from me. His eyes fixed on his sister's back as she walked towards the pool and over to Liam, who was chilling in a lawn chair. She settled in next to him and whispered something into his ear. He grinned and found my eyes with his. The thumbs-up from him made me blush.

Sheepishly, I cast my gaze in Kanoa's direction.

"Come on," he breathed.

Kanoa took my hand and pulled me into the house. I grinned in delight to know that his sister hadn't completely ruined the mood. And I was really curious where he was taking me.

Once upstairs, we went to a room at the end and slipped inside. It was masculine in decor, and that's about all I noticed because my eyes were fixed on Kanoa. He was flushed from the run, but he looked embarrassed too. "Is this okay? We were just getting to the good part...."

I laughed, my anxiety disappearing. He really was a hopeless dork just like me. "It's perfect."

I didn't want to risk any more interruptions. I grabbed him and kissed him—clumsy, awkward and so full of *need*. I'd been yearning for him for so long. I didn't care how unskilled I was. I just wanted to know what it was like to kiss a boy I liked.

There's a lot of sappy words I want to use to describe how it felt. I won't, because they would make you vomit. I will say that kissing Kanoa was everything I had ever dreamed of. It was better than swimming, even. I just wanted to crawl into that moment and live there forever.

Learning the art of making out with Kanoa is the sort of thing dreams (steamy, hot dreams) are made of. I stopped worrying about everything. He was beautiful. He was perfect. He was *mine*.

I got swept away in the moment. He didn't object at all when I went for the zipper on his jeans. I was operating solely on instinct, and that gave me a clear map for what to do. It wasn't like I was going to lose my virginity at a party where anyone could walk in at any moment. But I had been waiting to touch his gorgeous skin for way too long.

Kanoa seemed okay with that plan.

He did let out a yelp of surprise when I laid a slap across his bare ass, though.

"That was for standing me up," I explained and then petted the little hurt I'd given him.

There was a lot of stroking, a little licking and some very interesting gasping over the next few minutes. I'm not giving the details. All I'm going to say is that being gay rocks. For real.

As we lay there on the disheveled bed, curled up and catching our breath, I found myself feeling like I was ready to take on the world.

The dance was really a lot of fun. Kanoa looked amazing in the suit he wore for the occasion—a suit I looked forward to peeling him out of at some point. What can I say? Kanoa looks hot naked.

Liam and Aolani were obnoxiously adorable, laughing and joking the whole time. I still felt a twinge of jealousy looking at them, but it was muted. My feelings for Liam were still there, but they were pushed to the side by the incredible feelings that being with Kanoa filled me with.

Aolani's only comment on Kanoa going with me was, "About fucking time."

At first it was scary, basically announcing to everyone that I was gay. There were some haters at the dance. Zach gave me a look of utter disgust and then wouldn't look at me again. Others made some asinine remarks, but who cares about them? With Kanoa next to me, I was ready to take on the world.

Most people either ignored us or gave us approving nods. Even Jimmy was cool about it, saying he "figured" but smiling in a way that said it was all cool. Brian and his girlfriend Diana insisted on dancing with us.

Yeah, about that….. My only consolation was that Kanoa was almost as bad. Being an awful dancer isn't so embarrassing when your partner is just as awkward. And we were more interested in finding places to make out anyway.

At one point, Liam found me by the punch bowl. "Justin scores the hot senior," he said, smiling at me.

There was no way I could do anything but grin at him. I think my face had gotten stuck in smile-mode. It was freaking people out.

"Only because I have the best friend in the whole world."

"Well, yeah. Nice to see you acknowledge that."

I looked over to the table where Aolani and her brother were chatting. He said something that made her laugh that full-throated laugh of hers. I kind of liked her, to be honest—even if she was a man-stealing hussy.

"You seem to have gotten your own hot senior."

"Well, I have a pretty good friend too."

"How have you been? I've been kind of busy with swimming and Kanoa…."

Liam shrugged, a peculiar gleam in his eyes. "Not tonight, Justin. Lou doesn't get tonight."

That sounded bad, but I wasn't going to make him talk about it when he clearly didn't want to. "Okay…."

"Let's go get our picture taken, the four of us."

I went along with him, grinning at his manic demands for a picture. Kanoa and Aolani were retrieved and dragged over to the photographer. We took several, but my favorite was with me and Liam in back, our dates sitting in front of us. We had our arms around each other, grinning like the dopey idiots we were; two friends enjoying a big school dance.

CHAPTER 21

Hospitals are creepy places. They smell weird, they're full of diseases and death. There's this whole ugly feeling of misery around them. I had never spent much time in them before, but I had grown to loathe them. The fact that Liam was trapped in one only made me hate them more.

A week after the dance, his doctors had seen some things in their tests that they didn't like and had admitted him for *more* tests. That was two weeks ago, and they still wouldn't let him leave. I resented them for it. Liam was too full of life to belong in a hospital.

Only, with each passing day, that was less true. He slept a lot now and when he was awake, he still wasn't really Liam. Lou was beating him down.

I got off the elevator and quickly made my way to his room. I had some news for him, news that I knew would cheer him up.

Anna and Mike were there. I didn't know if they still worked. I knew they didn't sleep anymore. They were always there, always dealing with the doctors and nurses. They were with me, in the trenches fighting Lou.

Liam was sitting up when I came in. There were dark circles under his eyes. He gave me a friendly wave, though, like nothing at all was wrong. That made me smile. He hadn't even been strong enough to fake being okay in days.

"So, what's this big announcement my parents say you have?"

I looked to Anna and Mike, grateful they had let me be the one to tell him. "You're getting your bone marrow transplant," I told him.

His face scrunched up. "How…?"

"We're a match," I told him. "Doctors gave me the news today."

Liam stared at me. "Dude, that's…."

"It's nothing at all," I insisted.

Liam's eyes moistened. He wiped angrily at them and looked at his parents. "Could you give us a minute?"

"Sure hon," Anna said.

"We'll go hit the cafeteria," Mike told him.

Once they were gone, I went to sit beside him. I did my best to ignore all the *things* attached to him—the IVs, the oxygen tube, the things that went beep—the things that reminded me that Lou was coming for my best friend. I knew, rationally, that they were helping Liam, but I couldn't escape the feeling that what they were really doing was sucking the life out of him.

I took his hand. "It's really no big deal."

"Dude, it's a huge deal. It's not like giving blood."

I shrugged. "Don't care."

Liam smiled, a tear sliding down his cheek. "I really appreciate it, dude. I mean…. I mean, just I don't even know what to say."

"Liam, I've been trying to find something I can do to help. I'm lucky we're a match. It's pretty much a miracle."

He closed his eyes and collapsed back on the bed. "You just…. I don't…." He fiddled with the *thing* attached to his finger. "I think I'm done, Justin."

I felt my heart stutter to a stop. The world slipped out of focus for a second. "What?"

Liam looked at the ceiling, tears now slipping freely down his face and into his pillows. He looked so utterly exhausted. The toll of fighting Lou for so long had hollowed him out in ways that he kept so well hidden.

"I don't want any more procedures."

"But—"

"I don't want the fight anymore." He wiped at his eyes. "I know that makes me a quitter, but I'm just so tired."

He was always so strong, so positive. It was so easy to forget that he was just a guy my age, being slowly murdered over a period of years. To me, he was like a hero of legend. But I had also seen him naked—really naked, the sort where all of his vulnerabilities had been out in the open. I knew what his fight with Lou took out of him every day.

I had no right to ask him to keep fighting. I knew it was selfish of me to push him. But I just couldn't lose him. He was my foundation now.

"You can't let Lou win," I told him, hearing my voice crack. "You're too strong to give up."

Liam shook his head, his eyes sliding shut. "Lou and I have been slugging it out for years. I've given him a good fight, I gave it everything I had, but here I am, back in the hospital. I just don't have anything else to give."

"You've got me." He turned his face to me. "You can't die, Liam," I said, not caring to hide the tears on my face. "You can't. I need you too much." I felt raw, broken. "I love you, Liam, so don't you dare fucking die."

Liam didn't respond. He just looked at me for the longest time. My confession didn't seem to surprise or upset him at all. I didn't know what else to say. I knew we could beat Lou together, him and me, but he had to be willing to get back in the ring. He had to trust me.

"So, this is all just a plot to fill me with your genetic material?"

I choked out a sobbing laugh. "Yeah, that's it."

"Justin…."

"Please, Liam…. Please, just one more fight."

He squeezed my hand. "Okay, Tina. I'll do it for you."

I sniffled. "Don't call me Tina."

I was ready to do the procedure that day, but the doctors had doctor reasons why they needed to delay. They felt Liam needed to build up some strength, which sounded stupid to me. But of course, I'm not a doctor.

I had to badger my mom into signing the release form. She didn't like the idea at all. It took several doctors explaining the procedure to her and a tearful plea from Anna before she finally gave her consent.

Finally, the day came for me to report to the hospital to have my marrow sucked out. I wasn't nervous. I wasn't excited about it—I knew it was going to be a tough thing to do—but I was determined to kick Lou in the balls. My hatred for that son of a bitch was all the motivation I needed.

"You've got some mail," my mom said as I came into the kitchen.

"Huh?"

I never get mail. I picked up the legal-sized envelope and examined it. Even then it took me a minute to recognize the name of the studio that I had sent Liam's photo to. I'd forgotten all about it. Excited, I ripped it open and yanked out the letter.

"We are pleased to inform you of your first place ranking…."

I let out a whoop of delight and danced around the kitchen. My mom stared at me like I was insane. In that moment, I kind of was. It was so utterly perfect. It was exactly what I needed to get Liam motivated for the fight. He'd either be really excited at his win or he'd be utterly furious that I had entered his work without his permission. Either way, he would want to get out of that bed.

My mom dropped me off at the hospital. She wanted to stay, but she couldn't get the time off. I told her not to worry about it, that I'd be out for a while anyway. What I didn't tell her (because it would make her head explode) was that my boyfriend had promised to come by and feed me ice cream afterwards.

Kanoa was really proud of me for doing this, which was another huge plus. What seemed to me to be a no-brainer was to others this really big gesture. I understood it was a serious kind of thing to do, but really, who wouldn't do that for their best friend?

I rushed up to Liam's room. I wanted him to see the letter before they sedated him for the procedure. He was going to be featured in a magazine. There was also a fat check that I knew his family could use.

I skittered to a halt at the entrance to his room, my huge grin fading from my face as my world shattered.

Anna was crumpled in Mike's arms, sobbing and clutching to her husband. He held her and rocked her and mumbled nonsense words even as his own tears coursed down his face. I only saw that out of the corner of my eye, though. My attention was locked on the still form laying on the bed and the utter impossibility of the silence of the machines.

His hospital gown was askew like some nurse had tried to cover him after the paddles had failed to bring him back. Yes, there was a cart with paddles nearby. There were also various empty packets where sterile pads and needles had come from, all scattered around the floor, evidence of the final battle against Lou.

Liam was staring upwards, like he had fought to the very last to hold on, refusing to close his eyes on the world, refusing to give in. His face was utterly serene. He was beautiful.

And he was dead.

The world spun. I slumped against the doorway. There was no making sense of what I was seeing. There was no way this could be happening. We were winning. We were going to kick Lou in the balls and walk away laughing. We were going to share all of our dating stories. He was going to watch me take the trophy next year. He was going to get his own magazine feature. We were going to graduate together....

I stumbled away; delirious, unseeing, crushed. I don't know how it happened, but I found myself on a bench outside. Maybe I was hoping the open air would help me breathe. It didn't. I shook all over like a leaf caught in the wind. The image of Liam's still face burned into my mind, shredding every pathetic attempt I made to deny what I'd lost.

My phone rang. Like some sort of puppet, I picked it up. It was reflex.

"Hey, babe," Kanoa said. "Just wanted to wish you luck before they shoot you up with the happy drugs."

"Liam's dead." Even saying it aloud didn't help it make sense.

"Oh my God. Oh, baby.... Where are you?"

"On a bench." I was so cold inside.

"At the hospital?"

"Yeah."

"I'll be right there."

"Okay."

I knew how utterly stupid I sounded, like some kind of idiot child, but the shock had robbed me of the ability to think. I didn't mind the shock, though. In fact, I clung to the shock because I was terrified of what was coming after it.

A terribly dark cloud loomed on the horizon. I didn't think there would be anything left of me after that storm hit.

I don't know how long it was before Kanoa got there. Time had no meaning. But when he sat beside me and brought me into his arms, the storm swept over me. I broke into a thousand pieces and cried like a lost, hurt child.

He rocked me and told me everything would be okay. But he was wrong. Liam was dead. Nothing would ever be okay ever again.

CHAPTER 22

L iam's funeral was beautiful and terrible all at the same time. There were a lot of people in attendance—way more than I'd expected. Relatives, of course, filled a lot of the seats. But there were doctors and nurses from the hospital. There were also teachers and students from school.

I would not have been able to get through it if Kanoa had not been right there beside me, holding my hand through it all. He was a real hero, since he also had to comfort Aolani, who sat on the other side of him, gently sobbing.

My eyes were dry for the first time in days. I sat there, staring at the coffin as the service went on. Some stupid, crazy part of me kept hoping Liam would pop up and tell me it had all just been a really bad joke.

Of course, that didn't happen.

Mike got up and talked about his son. Or he tried. He kept breaking down, like when he talked about Liam's childhood fear that the Tooth Fairy would actually steal his teeth. And how he had liked to play Santa's elf in the hospital Christmas parties when he'd been a kid. Mike kept going, though. He wanted everyone to know how amazing Liam was. But anyone who knew him should have known that.

I wanted to get up there and tell them all about my friend, but I couldn't. I knew that the moment I tried to speak, my throat would seize up and I'd collapse. I hoped Liam would forgive me for being such a wuss.

Afterwards, at the grave, I ignored the priest and his meaningless words about eternal life and God's plan. I just stared at the casket. I kept my eyes on it as it was lowered into the ground. I watched as it was sealed into its concrete vault.

I couldn't move. I know how dumb it was, but I just wanted to see him safely tucked in. So I sat there long after everyone else had left. Kanoa, sweet, wonderful Kanoa, told me he'd wait for me in the car. He already knew me well enough to know I needed time.

Was there enough time in the world to deal with this?

I got out of the way as the workmen cleared away the chairs and the flowers. I watched them pour the dirt into the grave. That was covered with a blanket of sod, so it matched all the others. Now it was just one of the hundreds in the cemetery, a spot people would step over to get to their own loved ones. Would anyone see his marker and wonder about the sixteen-year-old boy who had died?

"God damn it, Liam."

My fingernails dug into my palms.

"How could you do this to me?" I breathed.

I wiped my eyes on my sleeve. Hurting and lost, I stared at the ground. For days I'd been trying to come to terms with Liam's death. I'd given up raging about unfairness, because Liam would have been the first to tell me that life isn't fair. Even the fury at Lou for taking him away hadn't lasted long.

Now I was struggling towards acceptance. Every time I came out of practice, I looked for him. Every English class, I stared over at his empty desk. I knew I needed to get over it, but I just had no idea how. The world without him didn't make sense.

I took a joint out of my pocket. I'd swiped it from his room when I'd gone over to help Anna and Mike pack things up. They were moving, going someplace that didn't remind them of Liam every day.

I lit the joint and sucked in the fumes and choked. "Shit, you really liked these things?" I asked him, not caring that I looked insane talking to myself.

I shook my head. "I got a letter from someone at the studio. They wanted to feature your photos in some sort of youth art gallery thing. When I told them about … what happened, they still wanted to go ahead. I put them in touch with your folks."

I took a second hit on the joint. I didn't like it any better on the second try.

"Your parents are going to use the prize money to pay down some debts and start over, so it looks like you helped them after all."

My throat was raw and scratchy. It had been for days. Convulsive crying had that effect on me.

"Kanoa came out to his parents. They're coping, though his grandmother is hoping it's a phase. Kind of like my dad, who thinks I'm not really gay, I'm just saying that to act out. Yeah, I told him to go to hell. You'd have been proud."

I'd hoped trying to talk to him like normal would help. It didn't. It just made his absence even more real.

I looked skyward, feeling the tears burning down my face. "Aw, shit, look at me, Liam. I'm here talking to a bunch of dirt. You see what you've reduced me to?"

I looked down at the bronze plaque with his name on it. "Brave and beloved son," I murmured. "That hardly covers it." I wiped my eyes again and pinched off the joint. "You were the most amazing, most incredible guy I've ever met. You changed my life. You changed *me.*"

I knelt down and moved the sod aside so I could bury the joint in the dirt near the plaque. It seemed like a fitting final gift.

"Liam…" I choked back a sob. I just knew if I gave into them I'd be come undone. "You were such an amazing person. It makes no sense that you…. And I…."

Those thoughts were too dark and I didn't want them overtaking me. "You were so brave, all the way to the end. You fought so hard, and I know you didn't want to. You did it because I made you promise...."

Breathe, I told myself. *Just breathe.*

"I won't ever forget you. Not ever. You were…. You were…." I found a little smile somewhere, hidden deep down inside my broken heart. "You were awesome."

The End

Please take a moment to check out these very worthy charities that help young people and their families dealing with cancer.

The Tyler Robinson Foundation helps families with the financial burdens that come with fighting this disease.

Teenage Cancer Trust focuses on improving the lives of teenagers and young adults battling cancer.

About the Author

I've been writing since I was fifteen, not that those stories will ever be allowed out of the dark hole I buried them in. I focused primarily on the Fantasy genre for the first two decades, occasionally diverting into modern fiction. In 2010, I embarked in a self-publishing career, focusing on the young adult novel genre. When I'm not writing, I am contributing to TheBacklot.com, a gay entertainment website.

You can follow me on Facebook and you can keep up to date with my works via Lightbane.com.

Also From Chris O'Guinn

    This is the story of me, Collin Murray, a bright, witty and charming L.A. teen who is cruelly transported to a small town in Iowa by parents who delight in my suffering. It tells the tale of my struggles against such obstacles as flannel, packs of bullies, lack of car, hoodies, crazy English teachers and vengeful former friends. It is an epic tale of survival in a savage denim wilderness.

Chris O'Guinn

Enjoy an excerpt from Exild to Iowa. Send Help. And Couture.

I got through the rest of my classes without any more drama, which I felt was a tremendous victory for me. My parents, being the wonderfully protective (re: controlling) people they are, had made a sweeping declaration that I would only go home with my brother. This would ensure I was not home alone, because we all know how insane it is to let a nigh-sixteen-year-old be at home alone for a couple of hours.

Is my bitterness showing again?

So, after classes, I found myself consigned to one of my least favorite places in the universe—the school gym. I could have gone to the library, but libraries sort of freak me out. All that quiet is just unnatural. So, even though I had some mild PTSD-y issues with the school gym, it was the preferable of the two.

I sat upon the bleachers, going over my homework half-heartedly and occasionally paying attention to the goings-on courtside. Unlike most boys my age (of my particular persuasion) jocks did nothing for me. You get tossed into enough Dumpsters, pantsed a few times and knocked around a bit, all by guys in jerseys, and the appeal wears off— or it did for me, anyway.

Still, they did look nice when they moved.

At some point, a now-familiar icy presence stole over me. I blinked and looked up at the darkness named Austin, surprised to find him there. The even stranger thing was the fact that he was now looking right back at me. That made me deeply uncomfortable and I had the irrational fear that he might think I was stalking him. I certainly had gaped at him enough in one day.

I resolved to focus on the fascinating events of pre-Christian Europe and not think so much about the miniature terrorist sitting a few seats up from me. I didn't want him to think I was in any way curious about him, after all, which I completely wasn't, and I didn't want him to think he needed to blow up my house or anything. It wasn't that I *liked* my house or anything, but it beat living in a cardboard box.

If only I could get over the feeling that he was boring holes into my back with his patented "the whole world needs to burn" glower.

I watched someone on the court pass the ball to someone else, who pranced around for some reason or another before passing the ball to yet another player, none of whom were my brother. I tried very hard to be supportive of Shawn, but there were some divides that even love could not bridge.

"Basketball fan?"

I blinked, trying to process the idea that the darkness behind me had spoken. It seemed like an odd thing for darkness to do, really—just strike up random conversation with a boy who was trying so very hard to not get into any more trouble.

"Er, not on purpose," I replied, risking a glance over my shoulder. "My brother…. He's, uh … a center…." I at least knew that much.

"Ah."

"You? Basketball groupie?"

"No. Dad's the coach."

"Oh, right."

There weren't a whole lot of places I could go with that awkward moment, which was probably wisest. After all, I was just starting off at the school (and not doing a very good job of it) and so it wasn't a really good idea to make nice with the resident sociopath, only he didn't really seem quite so crazy close up.

"Now, if they broke out into a song and dance routine, then I'd be interested," I volunteered for absolutely no justifiable reason.

There was a nervous silence as Austin turned my little comment over in his allegedly-murderous thoughts. "That would actually be sort of scary. I've heard the point guard, Justin, sing. It's not pretty."

I nodded and let it drop, not knowing where to take the painfully stalled conversation from there. My little "High School Musical" reference had fallen flat (which wasn't surprising) and I didn't know what else to say to someone who (possibly) harbored murderous impulses. It did not exactly make for good small talk.

"Of course, Zac Efron's not tall enough to be a basketball star either, though, so I suppose it all balances out in the end."

"Oh my God, did you just make an HSM reference?" I asked, shocked.

"You started it," Austin replied uncertainly.

"Oh my God! Who's your favorite? Troy? No, I bet it's Chad.... I mean, no, er.... Gabriella, right? I can't wait for HSM3. I'm dying to see it. I wonder if it will even play in this town."

Like a startled turtle, Austin hunched in on himself in the face of my excitement. His haunted gaze was inscrutable (which is to say, I had no idea if I had just ruined any chance of making a new friend or not) and his body language was completely closed off.

"Er ... sorry ... just ... didn't think anyone in this burg might have.... I didn't think I'd meet another fan ... or … guess you're not.... Okay, shutting up now."

I returned to my staggeringly boring pre-Christian Europeans, knowing I was beet-red from my embarrassment. My Irish heritage does not allow me to hide my humiliation well—or at all, really. Usually, I am able to keep my cool and not spazz out on someone, but after the day I had been having, the notion of finding someone with a shared interest was like chilled water down a parched throat.

"I liked Ryan, actually. The way he learned to stand on his own was awesome."

I had been spun around so many times at this point I was actually starting to feel a little dizzy. I bit my lower lip and stared blankly at the pages in front of me and debated my options. I could respond—roll the dice and see how many other ways I could mess this up. I could smile politely and go back to my reading, sort of close down the conversation in the most innocuous way possible. I could flee, making up some story about a forgotten errand.

They all had their advantages and disadvantages. I had just had such a rough day that the idea of being messed with once more seemed too much to bear. He could easily be yanking my chain, trying to lead me into saying something that he could use against me; but that didn't seem to make sense. Mr. Brooding Silence had not spoken to anyone in a while, by all accounts, so why would he strike up a conversation with me just to be a jerk to me?

I turned around, smiling a little and firmly reining in my hyperactive tendencies. I didn't want to send him running, after all. "My name's Collin," I introduced myself.

He nodded, apparently having gotten that bulletin. "Austin."

Awkward silence followed. I was in a death match with myself over what to not say, how to not say what I wanted to say and some odd concerns over how my hair looked after a long day in the hot and humid school. That all sort of tied up my tongue and left me unsure how to proceed.

Austin apparently had a degree in being taciturn, so he did not offer me a rope to pull me out of the pit I was in.

"Er, I liked Ryan too." Of course, I had a mad crush on Troy, but I can hardly be blamed for that. "He dared to be different."

Well, he dared to be queer, in my eyes, but I wasn't going to say that.

"I didn't try to blow up my old school," Austin blurted.

"Oh.... Huh?" Now I was totally lost. How had we gotten here?

"I know what people say," Austin told me quietly, his expression guarded. "But I didn't try to blow up my old school. That's not.... That isn't why I got transferred here."

Silence reigned for a moment while I processed that information and tried to figure out why he was giving it to me. It was nice to know, sure, but why did he care what I thought about him?

"Okay.... Good to know...." Wow, I failed at life sometimes. I had no idea what to say. How did one casually change topics after that, after all?

"Where did you come from?" Austin asked me.

"Mars," I replied. "Or, might as well be, as alien as I am around here."

Was that the barest hint of a smile I got from him on that?

"You don't look green from here."

"It's the lighting. Also, I work wonders with makeup." I told myself to absolutely not let my camp get out of control. I'd already been lame enough for one day. "But, no, actually, L.A."

"Where's that?"

I blinked and then saw yet another ghost of a smile on his face. And it was literally a ghost of a smile—the undead remnants of something that clearly had perished a long time ago.

"Funny man," I commented with a grin.

"Says the Martian."

"Fair point."

Austin was not relaxing, per se, but he was definitely growing more animated, which I hoped was a good sign. Though I could not pin down exactly why, I was drawn to him and I wanted to be able to be friends. The fact that it would kill any chance for improving my social standing was something that did not occur to me then.

We made small talk, which was painful and awkward, but kind of awesome at the same time. I could tell how out of practice he was with the whole talking thing and it was sort of sweet, really. I told him a little of L.A. and he volunteered absolutely nothing about himself.

I finally screwed up the courage to blurt out the question that had been lurking between us since his little declaration about not being a mad bomber. "So, why *did* you get transferred, then?"

"Huh?"

"Well, if you know what the rumors say, but you haven't corrected them ... what could the real reason be? It couldn't be worse than everyone thinking you're nuts. Why haven't you told people the real reason?"

Austin had a mild panic attack, his eyes going wider than I had yet seen them. I had apparently blitzed him with questions he had hoped to not have to answer for a while ... or forever. He stammered, folded his arms around his chest and closed down. It was frustrating and confusing and left me a bit at a loss for what to do.

No, I don't like bad boys and you're a terrible person if you were thinking that. I wasn't into him because he was troubled.... I was into him because he was interesting ... in a troubled way.

I had utterly lost track of practice, though, and my brother had inconveniently finished showering and was now calling for me. I was about to protest, but he had a look on his face which I recognized as "don't give me any crap" so I let Austin off the hook.

"See you around," I told the mysterious young man and went to see what had set Shawn off.

I was going to get an answer from Austin on that question though, at some point.

Coming Soon!

The night that Joaquin witnesses the fire in the sky was the last night of anything normal for him. His world of high school and football is completely upended as he comes face to face with an extraterrestrial being.

Thrace, as the alien calls himself, seems friendly enough. However, he has abilities that are far beyond human. And he comes with word that others of his race are already on Earth.

Joaquin's friendship with Thrace takes him into danger and chaos as he learns the terrible truth of why the aliens have come to Earth. He and his friends must find some way to help Thrace stop his people, or the human race will suffer the consequences.

The only thing that Joaquin now knows for certain is that our world will never be the same.

Enjoy an excerpt from Hybrids: Arrival!

Joaquin stopped jogging and gaped in amazement. Not only had the pilot miraculously survived, he was conscious and moving under his own power. The unlikely survivor hopped down from a pile of rocks and dusted himself off as if he had just taken a tumble on his ATV.

When he spotted Joaquin, he headed over. Joaquin turned his flashlight on the man and frowned as he took in the features of the strangest guy he had ever seen. He was tall, almost as tall as Joaquin. He was young, too. Joaquin thought he looked like a teenager, but of course that was ridiculous. What would a teenager be doing crashing to in the New Mexico desert? The object had been moving too fast to be anything a teenager might pilot.

His broad-shouldered physique was like something out of one of the magazines Joaquin had stashed under his bed. Dirty blond curls framed a flawless, angular face. It was the eyes, though, that told Joaquin there was something odd about this stranger. At first they seemed brown, but when he got a better look he was sure they were gold.

"Hello there." The stranger had a huge smile on his soot-stained face. "That was some crash, but fortunately there were no injuries. I'm going to have to ask you to move along though. This area is, um, restricted."

His voice was deep and melodic. The casual tone, though, gave Joaquin pause. It really was like the man was just out for a stroll in the desert at night instead of having fallen out of the sky. Joaquin was dumbstruck. He literally couldn't think of a thing to say.

"*Parlez-vous francais?*" the man said, trying a second time. His carefree smile waned a bit.

He wasn't wearing a flight suit or uniform or anything that might suggest where he came from. Instead he wore the remnants of some dark black

~ 214 ~

bodysuit that clung to him like spandex. It was torn and singed in several places, revealing glimpses of the pale skin underneath.

"W-Why are you speaking French?"

Joaquin's brain seized up on him. No human being could have walked away from a crash like the one that had just happened. But what did that mean? What could that mean? Joaquin dismissed the idea that he was dealing with something other than human. He lived with the comfortable certainty that there was no such thing as aliens. Unfortunately, skepticism aside, he was struggling to come up with a more plausible explanation.

"Oh, no reason, just thought I might be in Montreal."

Joaquin stared at him. "How does this look like Montreal?"

"Um…." The stranger bit his lower lip, looking flustered. "I'm, er, Thrace. Captain Thrace, that is. Captain Thrace, um, Harcourt. I'm in the armed forces."

Joaquin's jaw worked futilely for a moment. Finally, he managed to say, "You don't look old enough to be in the military."

"Er…." That flustered look came over the man again.

Joaquin's eyes narrowed suspiciously. "I have my phone here. Shall we call your C.O.?

"Call my…. Um, no, that isn't necessary."

Thrace fidgeted with his long, narrow fingers. Joaquin folded his arms. He had no idea what the guy in front of him was hiding. Had he stolen something? That seemed ridiculous. Teens stole cars for joy rides, not experimental aircraft. How would he have even gotten into the hanger where such a thing was kept?

The pile of debris from which Thrace had emerged shifted and rumbled. It wasn't that the debris was settling. It was more that something under all that rock was moving. Joaquin's first thought was that it was another survivor, but some of the rocks he saw moving were far too big for a human being to lift.

"What's that?"

"What's what?" Thrace asked with wide-eyed obliviousness writ on his face.

"That," Joaquin said, pointing at the shifting debris.

Thrace hardly spared a look over his shoulder. "That's nothing. But you really should move along. I, uh, need to report to my Z.O. and this is a, uh, no fly zone."

Joaquin actually cracked a smile. "You have no idea what you're talking about."

Thrace looked down at his toes. "Um…."

"Who are you? Really?"

"I can't tell you. I'll get in so much trouble. You really need to get out of here. Please?"

Joaquin was far too curious to budge. He folded his arms. "Not until I get an explanation."

Thrace sighed and slumped. "I'm an ELF."

Joaquin's smile faded into utter bafflement. "Excuse me?"

Thrace looked rueful for a moment and then he laughed; a merry, lilting sound. "It's what your people call us—Extraterrestrial Life Form. But ELF is shorter."

Joaquin nodded stupidly. "Extraterrestrial…. You're an alien?"

"ELF."

"Whatever. You're from space?" He felt himself shaking.

Thrace laughed some more. "Certain parts of it, yes."

"But …. That's.... That's not possible."

"And yet here we are."

"But you look human."

"Well, I think it's more that you look like us."

Joaquin tried to think of something profound to say, but he was too shell-shocked. "Uh, Roswell is south of here…. Maybe you're lost?"

Another strangely infectious laugh filled the night air. "No, I'm not one of the Cartusians. I'm actually here to—" He stopped as the rubble made more obvious noises, huge boulders shifting aside. "Well, that's annoying. I'll be right back."

"Huh?"

"You really need to get out of here."

"What are you talking about?"

But the stranger did not answer. Instead, the impossible man did something that so totally offended Joaquin's sense of reality that he became convinced this was all some sort of hallucination. The blond man in front of him pushed off from the ground and *flew*.

As if that wasn't strange enough, something straight out of science fiction emerged from the rubble. It looked just like a flying saucer from the old movies, only this one was much smaller—about as wide around as a car. It tilted and wobbled as it hovered in the air, its disk-shaped frame unsteady from the crash. A series of blue and red lights dotted its shell, blinking erratically. Its surface was scored with char marks and hundreds of dents; the silvery skin was so buckled in some places that Joaquin could see the machinery underneath.

It didn't look big enough to have a human-sized pilot, but that didn't really mean anything, not on a night like the one Joaquin was having. He might have found himself in the middle of an alien turf war, for all he knew.

The damage to the saucer only delayed it for a few spare seconds, though. A pair of cannons appeared out of its upper fuselage and targeted Thrace. The ELF looped through the air gracefully, easily avoiding the blasts of green energy that came at him.

Joaquin knew he should run back to the mine, get his truck and get as far from this insanity as he could. A pitched battle between an alien—or ELF or whatever—and a flying saucer was not something he should be involved in. Yet he remained rooted to the spot as surely as if his feet were stuck in cement. There were simply too many mind-boggling things occurring, depriving him of the necessary brain capacity to move his feet.

Instead, he brought up his phone and took a quick video of the impossible scene. In seconds, he'd forwarded it to Sylvia. He did that more out of reflex than thought. He shared everything with her, after all—even things that simply couldn't really be happening.

Thrace retaliated against his attacker by dive-bombing it and slamming into it with both fists. The force of those massive impacts sent out shockwaves that jarred Joaquin's teeth. How could the man—this ELF—survive such stunning collisions? How could anyone?

The saucer's hide seemed impervious to such brute force, though. After a dozen thunderous attacks, the saucer was not noticeably damaged. Thrace changed tactics. He paused in midair and held one hand over his head. His youthful face scrunched up in concentration. In moments, bright crackling energy, like lightning, gathered in his grip. It was like he was a pagan god, wielding primal forces with the ease of thought.

Thrace danced away from another barrage of green energy blasts as if they were a mere nuisance. He then hurled a bolt of lightning from his hand like Zeus himself. It arced down, heading for one of the gaps in the saucer's armor. It would have struck true, but the disk-like craft did a barrel roll to protect itself. The arc of lightning bounced off the silver hide and grounded harmlessly.

A strange sound filled the air as both combatants adjusted position. It was the unmistakable sound of Thrace's musical laughter. He was *enjoying* this.

Sylvia responded with lightning speed. *WTF? Is this some kind of joke?*

Wish it was. GTG, aliens attacking. C U later if I don't die.

Made in the USA
San Bernardino, CA
14 May 2014